FROM BARS TO BALLROOMS

The Time Orb Series Book II

CALLIE BERKHAM BERKHAM

From Bars to Ballrooms:
The Time Orb Series Book II
Copyright © Callie Berkham 2020
Cover design by Gabrielle Prendergast
Published 2021 by DCF Books
ISBN: 978-0-9945011-2-7

DCF Books
CPA Calcium, 4545 Flinders Highway, Calcium, Qld, 4816
ABN 36069542904

CHAPTER 1

Izzy pushed the keyboard away and sat back with a harrumph. She'd been so excited when she'd started writing her new science fiction series. But that was before she saw Abby and Iain's love for one another firsthand.

Since Izzy's return from eighteenth-century Scotland, leaving her sister wedded to the love of her life, the Laird Iain MacLaren, all she could think about was true love and writing romances.

She had even read every romance she could find in the library, but the novels set in early nineteenth-century England lingered in her head the longest. She was drawn to the Georgian era. She liked the fashions and the manners of that time—they resonated with her. It amused her that, although it was never talked about in polite society, many people of that time had physical relationships before marriage.

However, she loved the idea that women were expected to be virgins before marriage. Wasn't that what she was doing? Waiting for Mr Right? Virginity wasn't something to hide back then, as if it were something to be ashamed about. Not like in modern times. She snorted. She wasn't a twenty-three-year-old virgin by choice really—she just hadn't met anyone she wanted to take that step with.

She'd been working on her first-ever romance novel for a week and, while she had written five chapters, they were hollow and unemotional. She couldn't get into the heroine's head. If she'd never experienced what the heroine felt, how could she write the necessary emotions?

And the hero?

How was she supposed to know what he was thinking? She'd never been able to read the minds of any of the men she'd dated. In fact, she'd never understood any of them, let alone known what their body language meant. It was as if there were secret rules to dating that she wasn't aware of.

She stared, unseeing, at the Word document on the screen. No matter how much she researched, she just couldn't picture how people really talked and acted in the early nineteenth century. In her head she knew they couldn't always have had perfect manners—they were people after all, and all people had faults, tempers, beliefs they held dear. Siblings would fight, children would sulk, and couples would surely quarrel.

And there were some people in the world one couldn't be nice to no matter what the rules were.

She saved and closed the document on her computer and eyed the file she had named *Carolyn's Story*. Scrunching up her face, she jabbed a key and deleted the folder. Picking up her hairbrush, she pulled it through her long blonde hair as she paced the room.

Maybe she should set the story in a different time. Maybe a time when there were white knights in shining armor racing around the country saving damsels in distress. If only those brave, strong, sexy men still existed; men who thought staying faithful to one woman was honorable.

Not likely.

Men of her time expected sex. Somehow it had become a given that if a couple dated x number of times, they would go through the steps leading to the bedroom. Sometimes couples had sex after their first date, maybe even before.

She wondered if there was something wrong with her. She always shied away from anything more serious than kissing at the end of a date. Even with her fiancé, the man she'd thought she loved, the man she'd thought she'd grow old with.

She gave a shake of her head, trying to rid her mind of the memory. Nope. It was stuck there, and once again she had to replay it.

Rodney, standing in the hallway, refusing to enter her apartment.

"No, Izzy, I won't be staying. I came to tell you I'm breaking off our engagement. I thought I could wait for you, but I can't, and before you hear it from someone else, you should know I'm seeing Sandra now."

Izzy had stared at him, trying to make sense of his words. He was with Sandra? *He's breaking up with me? Is that what he said?*

She looked down at her shaking hand. She twisted the ring, trying to take it off her finger. "Sandra?"

"Yes, and you can keep the ring."

He'd left her standing there still twisting the stupid ring, too shocked by his revelation to even cry.

Rubbing her head with both hands to try to erase the memories, Izzy decided she needed some fresh air. She grabbed her notebook and a pen. She needed a change of scenery.

Not five minutes later, Izzy called out from the top of the stairs before making her way down to the basement. "Hey-o."

It wasn't a scary basement—with so many lights, that was

CALLIE BERKHAM BERKHAM

never going to be a problem. She just thought it bad manners to turn up without prior warning.

"We're down here," her sister Max said, raising her voice only enough for it to reach the top of the stairs.

Izzy made her way down to find Max and their brother, Garrett, looking at something on the bench.

"What ya doin'?"

Garrett frowned and shook his head at Izzy's choice of words. He hated the way she didn't speak correct English. He thought it lazy and believed that, as a writer, Izzy had a responsibility to talk well. She couldn't help it. He was just too easy to ruffle.

Max mussed Izzy's hair while she spoke. "We're trying to figure out if the orbs can also be used as communication devices."

Backing off, Izzy patted her hair back into place. "I'm not a dog."

Max grinned. "No. But you're as cute as a golden retriever and I just can't keep my hands off your hair."

She made a movement to do it again, but Izzy ducked out of the way and faced Garrett. "So, have you worked it out?"

"No."

Izzy turned to Max, who shook her head, short dark hair flipping onto her face. She pushed it back. "If the devices can be used to communicate, we can't figure out how."

"I don't think they can," Garrett said. "I've read and reread the journals a hundred times, and I can't find any mention of Mom and Dad communicating with anyone else while they traveled."

"They didn't," Bree said.

Max furrowed her brow. "Where did you come from? I didn't even hear you come down the stairs."

Their cousin grinned. "I learned a long time ago if I wanted to take pictures of wildlife, I had to learn not to make

4

a noise sneaking up on them. I guess it's natural now. So, what are you all up to anyway?"

"We were wondering if Mom and Dad left out some info that we could use."

"Let's not talk about our parents." Garrett pushed off from the bench and walked to the stairs. "I still can't believe they time traveled, and Abby is living in the past in Scotland, for Pete's sake. It's too much."

He plonked up the stairs, still muttering to himself.

Bree chuckled and slid onto a stool.

CHAPTER 2

S trolling around the garden, Izzy tried to look as if she were deep in thought, while keeping an eye on the hallway, which she could see through the sitting room's French doors. Max always thought she was the boss. Even if Abby was around, Max always seemed to have the last say in everything. It had never bothered Izzy before, but now that she really wanted something, Max stood in her way. She snorted. Well, it was about time Izzy took control of her life.

Max finally made an appearance and turned her head to look through the sitting room. Izzy ducked down and picked a little clover daisy, hoping Max thought Izzy hadn't seen her.

When Izzy stood up, Max was gone, and she quickly made her way back down to the basement. Blast. The orbs were gone from the bench. Where had she put them?

Having searched the entire basement, Izzy stood in front of an empty shelving unit positioned against the back wall. Looking about, she noted tools, old broken ornaments, and papers strewn on the benches and stuffed into other shelves that could have been placed in the empty unit. "Why are you empty? And why do you look very much like the unit in Abby's castle's pantry?"

Her imagination ran away with her then. Could this be the entrance to a secret room? Orb forgotten, she shivered in excitement and ran her hand down the sides of the unit. Nothing. How did Jannet open the one in Iain and Abby's castle? She dragged a chair over and climbed up on it, so she could reach the top. But nothing was there either.

Kneeling, she examined the bottom, where she stuck her flat hand in the gap and carefully moved it along the floor. Ha, wheels. Bobbing back onto her feet, she moved to the side and pushed. At first it wouldn't budge, but she pushed again, and it squeaked as it rolled aside, revealing a door. Izzy giggled with excitement. Her parents must have enjoyed keeping so many secrets. What else would she find?

"Time to find out," she whispered and opened the door.

Row upon row of clothes from all different periods in history hung from rails, each about twelve feet long. She squinted. Shelves lined the back wall, jam-packed with boxes of who knew what.

"Wow. This is some wardrobe," Izzy gasped. She hurried down the rows of amazing costumes for men and women until she finally found what she was looking for in row seventeen.

Izzy spent the next hour going through the racks of nineteenth-century clothes and trying on different outfits.

She settled on a lovely lime-green day dress but couldn't do up all the buttons at the back. "No wonder they had people to dress them." Giving up, she let out a breath of air and pulled on a dark green coat. The smallest hat she could find was a bonnet that covered her entire head. She tied the green ribbon under her chin in a loose bow. Ugh, that would get annoying after a while.

She found a pair of dark green slippers that didn't look as

if they would stand much wear but, determined to look the part, Izzy slipped them on. They were a little tight, but she had no intention of walking far in them anyway.

Spinning around in front of the mirror, she stopped and beamed at her reflection and thought she would ask Garrett to take some photos of her. Maybe she could use one on the cover of her book when it was finished.

Izzy decided to stay in her costume while she spent the rest of the morning in her father's study, searching her parents' journals for any mention of the early nineteenth century. They had the photographs and writings of the history of the time, but nothing she could use to persuade Max to give her the white orb. She piled the journals up on her father's desk and sat back on the chair.

"I thought I was the only one here," Bree said, entering the room. "Hey, you found the wardrobe room."

Izzy leapt onto her feet and eyed Bree. "You knew about it? Why didn't you tell us?"

Bree took a step back. "Don't get all het up about it. I was going to tell you when you all decided who was going next."

Izzy clicked her tongue. "You could have told us before now, though."

"I'm sorry."

"Any other secrets?"

Bree grinned. "Maybe."

"So, are you going to tell me?"

"That would be too easy. I think it's more fun if you find out for yourself."

Izzy frowned. Bree was always a bit eccentric. Izzy imagined her fiery red hair was the culprit— that maybe it was so hot, it had burned her brain. She eyed her cousin. Although Bree was being downright annoying at that moment, Izzy couldn't resist a game.

She smiled. "Another secret room?"

"Warm."

"So, not a room then." A thought popped into Izzy's head. "A secret hiding place!"

Bree laughed. "Yes."

Izzy flitted around the room, checking and rechecking every wall, every bookshelf, and every book, with Bree saying if she was hot or cold. The only time Bree said 'warm' was when Izzy was near the desk. She plopped onto the chair and eyed the messy desk. She snorted. "Of course."

Bree sat on the chair opposite and said, "Warm."

Izzy ran her hands over and under and down the sides but still found nothing. Taking out the drawers one by one, she checked every part but found nothing there either. "Darn it. There has to be something."

"You're really warm, Iz. Keep looking."

Thinking she had nothing to lose, Izzy twisted every drawer handle. Nothing. She turned the handle on the wide, shallow drawer across the front of the desk. *Click.* "Ah ha," she exclaimed, and beamed at Bree.

Bree laughed. "Hot."

Izzy bent down and gazed under the drawer and saw to her delight that a small box had appeared in the left-hand corner. "Ha, I should have been a spy."

"Scorching—and yes, you would have made a great spy."

Opening the little door, Izzy pulled out a small book. It was smaller than the rest and had a hard, solid, blue cover with the swirly title *Trust Forever*.

Flipping through it, she found the pages to be full of people's names with numbers beside them, their addresses, and time periods. Her heart quickened. They had to be Mom and Dad's contacts. And from the title of the book she concluded they were people her parents trusted. She gave a little shake of her head and let out a laugh. Of course, they would have found friends. She hoped they had someone in the early eighteen hundreds.

On the first page her mother had written: *Set the orb to the year, country code and contact number*. Izzy couldn't remember the orb having anywhere to set the year. Max and Garrett had been studying it. Would they know about the settings? She snorted. She wasn't about to ask them. She eyed Bree. "Do you know how to use the orb?"

Bree nodded.

"Where are the settings?"

"On the bottom."

"You could have told us about this booklet and how to set the orb, you know."

"I could have, and I would have if you never found it, but honestly?" She shrugged. "This is way more fun."

"For you, maybe," Izzy grumbled.

"Don't be like that. I've lived by myself for years and I hardly get to spend time with you guys. Where do you want to go?"

"Early eighteen hundreds." She looked at Bree. "For research."

Bree waved her hand at the book. "Well then?"

Izzy read through the next pages. They contained time periods arranged by dates, so it was easy to find what she was looking for, but only one date appeared there. It was 1811. She smiled as she touched the writing with her finger. At least it was in the Georgian period, but more precisely, Regency. The date represented a page number. Izzy quickly flipped through the book to the page stated.

She widened her eyes at Bree. "A duke?" She grinned. "Cool."

She read the address in what she thought was an English upper-class voice. "His Grace, the Duke of Chodstone, K. G.,

Chodstone House, Manchester Square, London. Birth name: James Porter, 56."

She wondered what the letters K. G. stood for and decided she'd have to look them up before she left.

"Thank goodness," Izzy mused. "That should make things easier."

"Izzy?" Garrett's voice floated through the walls.

"Rats. I was supposed to go riding with him." She ripped out the page with the address and stuffed it in her pocket. "Don't say a word."

Bree smiled and, using her finger, zipped her mouth closed.

A door slammed, and Izzy jumped. She stopped and listened. "I hope that was Garrett leaving the house and not Max coming back."

"I'm sure it was Garrett. So, are you going to go?"

"If I can find the orb. Max hid it, the rat."

Bree pulled something out of her bag. "This one?"

"How did you...? Never mind, give it to me."

"Sure."

With trembling hands, she took the orb and examined every surface. A gold leaf stood out a little on the bottom. She pushed it and a small square opened. Using her fingernail, she turned the tiny dial until it clicked on 1811, then noted a dial next to it. What was the code for the United Kingdom? She quickly used her cell and, once she'd found the code, clicked the dial to forty-four. "What's the last dial for?"

Bree grinned. "Change it to fifty-six, that's the number of the contact."

Izzy narrowed her eyes at Bree, she had a feeling her cousin wasn't telling her everything she needed to know. However, that was the number beside the duke's name in the book so she turned the dial to fifty-six.

Shutting the leaf door and inhaling deeply, she said, "This is it."

Bree smiled, and Izzy twisted the top of the orb until the leaves united like Abby had said she had done. The central spire rose.

Her weight lightened, and as if her body were a gentle wave, she floated. Up or down or around, she didn't know, but a moment later, she fell gently onto solid ground. Her legs were still weak, and she crumpled to her knees before falling back on her bottom. She peered at a horse drawn carriage pulling away from where she had just landed. She shivered. Another second sooner and she would have landed right on top of the carriage.

❧❦❧

EDWARD CAVENDISH, EARL OF WELLSNEATH, STEPPED OUT of White's and plopped his top hat on his head. He enjoyed fashion and much preferred his top hat to the military bicorne he wore when serving as an officer on the Spanish Peninsula.

His driver stopped the hooded landau within inches of the sidewalk before Edward could begin to dwell on the war that had taken his brother's life.

Edward held his breath as he stepped over the malodorous muck on the street and up into the carriage.

If he had his way, he'd stay with the company of gentlemen all night and not go to the soirée his mother had all but blackmailed him into attending. Emotional blackmail was the worst kind of extortion, he thought. Women were adroit at it, especially his mother.

Why his mother insisted they leave their country estate and return to London, he couldn't imagine. He'd enjoyed a particularly successful season up until his mother issued the directive that saw them travel to London during winter, instead of spending Christmastide at his country estate.

He placed his hat on the seat beside him and tapped the roof with his cane. The cane he still used—though he didn't really need it anymore—came in handy when socially-climbing mamas cornered him with introductions to their daughters, expecting him to dance with them. Complaining of his war injury kept them at bay, most of the time.

He also kept it as a reminder of the battle that saw him shipped home.

Now he was on his way to a soirée as if none of that had happened. He was supposed to enjoy his life, marry a suitable wife, and produce heirs.

Oh, he understood the requirement and had stepped up to the chopping block—if not eagerly then at least, he hoped, honorably. People of his type, people of the gentry, had no say in the course of their lives. Marriage was a way of joining titles and lands, a way of ensuring futures for their offspring, and Edward had left it up to his mother to find a suitable wife, one whose fortune would save their declining estates from his late father's neglect.

He knew whom his mother had in mind. The widow Lady Vera Cavendish. Her first husband had been a baron. Thomas, Edward's brother, was to have been her second husband, and as he'd been the heir to an earldom, she would have gained the title of countess. Her substantial fortune from her marriage with the affluent baron was well-known in the *ton* circle. And so was her ambition of a suitable title.

Edward smiled. Thomas was smitten with her the moment he saw her. And at first, Edward was happy for him, happy that a woman of such beauty would set on his brother. But once Edward became more fully acquainted with her and her flirtations, he had tried to talk Thomas out of the match.

In hindsight, he should have known better. It only made

Thomas more adamant about his love for Vera. He set a date to marry Vera and treated her son as his own. Edward shook his head. Thomas had been taken from them too soon.

He sat back against the cushion with a harrumph of defeat. He supposed Vera was a more suitable match than an innocent, starry-eyed debutante. Young women dreamed of love matches, but Vera knew the way of the finer class. She understood marriage was a contract and love had no place in contracts. As the widow of a baron, she also understood a step up the ranks would see her children's futures assured.

Love had no business in suitable matches, and the very thought of a love match had perished when Edward was seventeen years old.

The carriage had only just turned into Fleet Street when the driver shouted, "Woah, wo there." And the carriage jerked to a stop.

"What in—" But Edward's curse stalled as he opened the door and stared at a woman huddled on the ground, covering her head with her arms. She must have been the reason for the sudden stop.

CHAPTER 3

I zzy's head was full of cotton wool and her eyes, which she knew she had opened, couldn't see anything but glittering stars. She thought since it was daytime when she left the basement, she would arrive during the day. She blinked into the night. Blast.

With the clouds dissolving in her mind, awareness of the aroma surrounding her made her eyes water. She covered her nose and mouth with her hand. What was that? It smelled like open sewage with dead animals decomposing in it. And, she had the awful thought, she was sitting in it.

She quickly put the orb in her small purse and tried to stand up without touching the ground with her hands. Vibrations rolled under her. Someone shouted something incomprehensible. Izzy blinked and turned her head, and her eyes widened in fear. She gasped. Four horse's legs pranced within inches of her as she put her arms over her head and shrank back as far as she could go.

Strong hands grabbed her from behind, scooping her up by her armpits and flinging her around until she stood on the side of a road. The large hands turned her until she came face to chest with a man.

He removed his hands, but his warm handprints remained on either side of her waist. She lifted her eyes but quickly lowered them again. The man who had just saved her life vibrated anger. His black brows drew together, shading even blacker eyes that shot knives into hers. His mouth was a long, tight line.

"Are you all right?" he asked.

"I... I think so." Izzy screwed up her nose at the dreadful smells still assaulting her. Her stomach roiled. *What is that stench?* She inspected the area. A carriage rolled down the other side of the wide street. The manure from the great hulking horses would be one cause; another would be the dogs sniffing in and out of the shadows and relieving themselves everywhere.

She took in the man in front of her. He was the perfect image of tall, dark, and handsome. A hunk in any time period, dressed in perfect Regency attire and, by the look of the luxurious black waistcoat her eyes were glued to, he was a wealthy gentleman. She lifted her eyes over the pale blue cravat but, not wanting to look at him again, averted her gaze to her surroundings.

The man shifted his feet but didn't move away as he turned his face to the man driving the carriage. "Did you not see this lady?"

"No, m'lord. I don't know where she came from. She appeared out of nowhere."

The man grazed his eyes over Izzy, and the way they seemed to take in every inch of her had her nerve endings humming and her chest seething. *How dare he look at me like I'm a much-awaited meal?* An excited shiver ran down her backbone and she frowned at her ridiculous reaction.

Quickly turning away from him, Izzy scanned her

surroundings, not that she could see much. The streetlights cast only a small, soft glow.

They were on a corner, standing outside what appeared to be a large store.

She looked up and read the plaque on the red brick wall. *R Waithman, Linen Draper.*

By her parents' notes she should have arrived near their friend's house, not in the middle of what could only be a business district.

"No one would suggest this lady is a wallflower. She is not someone who blends into her surroundings so well that one cannot see her."

The driver glanced at Izzy. "No, my lord."

Izzy's attention snapped back to the man. *My lord?* The man was definitely titled. A duke? No, the driver would have said 'Your Grace'. Maybe a viscount or an earl or a marquis. *Nice.*

"Where are we?" Izzy asked, a little in awe.

His brown-black eyes pierced hers as he swept his hand down the street. "This is Fleet Street."

Although she tried not to, Izzy couldn't help scrunching up her nose at the stench surrounding her. The man, straight out of a Georgette Heyer novel, leaned in toward her. His scent, while not completely masking the smells, was much more pleasant.

Her nose relaxed, but at the same time, her body tensed. She stepped back but immediately wished she hadn't. With an effort, she stopped her hand from moving up to cover her nose again. She would have to get used to the stench sooner or later.

The hunk frowned as he looked her up and down.

She remembered then she had worn a day dress. Not the right thing, by the way he narrowed his eyes at her lovely dark green coat and pale green dress. As if reminded her coat wasn't as thick as it should be for an English winter night, she pulled it tighter around her.

He flicked his gaze in all directions and she wondered if he was looking for someone. *Oops.* She could almost hear his thoughts. No respectable woman would be out in the streets at night in that time. Actually, Izzy doubted respectable women ever went about on their own. They always had chaperones, didn't they?

Izzy bent her head and stared at the toes of her slippers. Drizzly rain began to fall on and around her. *Great.* She shivered and thought how stupid she was for not wearing something warmer. She had been to England before and should have remembered how cold and wet it could get in winter, but how was she to know what season in 1811 she would land?

He placed his fingers under her chin and tilted her head back. She blinked up at him, but she wasn't blinking away the remnants of the brief shower; she was fighting back the tears that threatened and burned her eyes. She thought she had every good reason to burst into sobs. She was alone after all, and stupid to have arrived there at night. Not only that, but the stupid orb had landed her right in front of a moving carriage nowhere near her parents' friend's house.

She gazed at her rescuer.

His jaw tightened.

Izzy didn't blame him for being angry. She was too. It was wet and cold, and he looked like he was on his way out—probably had a date with some aristocratic lady. And now she had made him late.

A large carriage passed. He glanced up as it slowed but kept his head down as if he didn't want to give his identity away. He also turned Izzy away so only her back could be seen by the inhabitants of the coach. She couldn't help smiling at his thoughtfulness. He was protecting her, protecting her reputation.

If they recognized him or his carriage, his reputation probably wouldn't be in jeopardy. Oh, he would be the talk of the society pages, but being a man, he could get away with things a woman couldn't. Izzy had to remember women were expected to be pure and above any hint of scandal.

As her eyes flicked to his, she stepped back and straightened her back to let him know she wasn't some kind of strumpet. She smiled. "I'm sorry, but I seem to be lost."

"A lady such as yourself shouldn't be out at this hour alone. Where are your parents? Your guardian? Or at the very least, your lady's maid or companion?"

"I don't have any of those things."

She rubbed the side of her head, trying to think of a plausible excuse, but found none.

Casting his concerned eyes over her flaxen hair, he appeared to look for some injury that might explain her confusion.

"Are you an American?"

Izzy nodded dumbly. "Yes, yes, I'm American."

The furrows between his brows deepened. "I was under the impression even Americans were escorted by their parents, or guardians, or ladies' companions."

He made it sound like he was asking a question and Izzy had nothing to say to that.

Gazing at her surroundings, she groaned quietly at her stupidity. She peered into her reticule. A wide smile broke out on her face as she brought out the page of notepaper.

"A guardian, yes, yes. I do have a guardian. That's where I was going."

She hoped the duke wouldn't mind her saying he was her guardian.

"You forgot you had a guardian? Have you hit your head, mayhap?"

Her hands inadvertently went to her head. "No... that is, I don't know." She shrugged. "Who knows? I might have."

A small tic in his jaw had her wondering if he really did think she was mad. She probably sounded crazy. Even though she tried to match his formal way of speaking, she knew she would seem completely alien by comparison with the women of his time.

"Surely American women don't wander around streets alone."

"No, we don't, it's just that I... um... the coach I traveled here in was going to go in the opposite direction to my destination and I didn't know anyone in... um... Piccadilly." She said the first place that popped into her head.

Another carriage drove past. He glanced at the open door of his carriage and then at his driver, who had a worried look about him.

"I will take you to your guardian."

Izzy frowned at the covered carriage. Women weren't supposed to be alone with men and especially, if they hadn't even been introduced. She had no idea who he was. He might dress like a gentleman, but he might be a cousin to Jack the Ripper.

"Ah, nope. That's not a good idea. I know how things work here. It would be improper without my having a chaperone." She tilted her head toward the coach. "If I get in there with you, I would be ruined." Her wide eyes questioned him. "Wouldn't I?"

The corners of his mouth quivered with a suppressed smile.

"Only if someone of note saw us, and I have no intention of allowing that to happen. However, if we continue to stand out here so all and sundry can see us, we are already ruined."

One half of her wished he wasn't standing so close, but the other half was thankful for his scent in her nostrils. She pulled out a piece of paper from her reticule. "If you could just point me in the direction I need to go, I'd be... um... much obliged."

She hoped she sounded aristocratic. Gazing at the paper, she said, "Where's Manchester Square?"

He raised a black eyebrow. "Is that where you live?"

"It's where I am going to live. So, if you could point me in the direction?"

"Are you new to London?"

"No... um... yes." *Nitwit.* "Yes. It's my first time."

He bent his head slightly and raised his dark brows. "You don't sound very certain."

Was he playing with her? Or didn't he want to show her where to go? She was a stranger and, in 1811, he was way above her social status. Maybe he sensed that and had decided she was too much trouble. Maybe he thought she wasn't worth spending any more time on.

A flash of anger passed through her. She might not have purple blood running through her veins, but she was human and surely that at least deserved some respect. "Can you show me the way or not?"

He straightened to his full height and, his eyes darkening with what could only have been fury at her question, gazed down his long nose at her.

She stood her ground, but a hesitancy made her bite her bottom lip. She realized women didn't talk to men like that in the eighteen hundreds.

He seemed about to say something but tightened his mouth. His glare turned to open curiosity, as if she were a puzzle, he wanted to solve.

"I will take you. I am going in that direction."

She glanced into the dark interior of the coach. She knew from the books she had read that traveling alone with a man wasn't seen as the thing to do. She twisted her fingers together. Standing around talking to a gentleman without a chaperone was wrong too, though. The last thing she wanted was to be the center of gossip. She had to keep a low profile or people would start to ask questions, questions she couldn't answer. Or if not that, she would bring shame onto her soon-to-be friend before she had even met him.

Izzy couldn't mistake the humor in his eyes at her worried look.

"Mayhap, it will calm you if I sit above." He pointed to the high seat.

She thought about that. "Yes, that might be better."

"Good." He pulled a folded blanket out, flipped it open and placed it on the bench seat. Holding her elbow, he helped her into the carriage. "Sit there." He pointed to the covered seat.

Izzy grimaced. Her back of her dress was wet with who knew what and she understood the need for the blanket, but it was so embarrassing.

Once she was seated, he asked, "What is your name?"

"Elizabeth, Elizabeth Davis."

"Are you the oldest daughter?"

"No, why?"

His eyebrows dipped in confusion. "I need that information to know how to address you." He bowed. "Lady Elizabeth."

He had obviously decided she was a lady, though why he would, Izzy had no idea. But she knew if she were the oldest daughter, he would have addressed her as Lady Davis. They had so many children back then—heh, *now*—they had to have a way of differentiating the oldest, although she had no idea why they would want to do so.

She liked being called Lady Elizabeth, so she wasn't going to disabuse him of that notion. Men treated ladies far better than people they saw as their underlings.

Once she'd settled on the seat, the carriage shivered as Edward sat down and the driver's astonished voice floated down to Izzy's ears. "My lord?"

"Manchester Square."

Unable to stop herself, Izzy poked her head out of the window trying to see as much as she could as they passed the streetlights. Her heart missed a beat. She was really in England in 1811. She was really being driven to the house of her guardian by the most handsome man she'd ever laid eyes on. His brooding, dark looks took her breath away, and not in the same way the stench did, either. He was altogether too sexy. She would get used to the smells of nineteenth-century London, and she looked forward to becoming accustomed to the manners of the era.

This is certainly my type of place.

The driver's voice floated from above. "My lord?"

"Huh?"

The gentlemanly hunk sounded as if he'd either been in deep thought or had fallen asleep. They hadn't been traveling all that long, so Izzy assumed his mind was on something other than their surroundings. A tingle coursed down her backbone at the thought that he might have been thinking about her.

"We have arrived at Manchester Square."

"Oh, of course, yes. Good man. Stop here."

Once the driver had pulled as far to the side of the road as he could, Edward jumped down and opened the carriage door.

Curiosity lit his dark eyes and Izzy couldn't help but stare up at his well-formed face. Sure, his nose was a little longer and straighter than most hunky models, but she liked it. It only enhanced his regal stature. And the deep philtrum, the beautiful vertical groove joining his nose to his mouth. That mouth, with a thin upper lip but a fuller, inviting lower lip.

"What is the number, Lady Elizabeth?"

Izzy frowned in confusion for a second then brightened in understanding. She straightened the scrunched-up notepaper she must have held in her hands all the way and looked at it. "There is no number—it just says Chodstone House."

He blinked. Bewildered. "That cannot be. Mayhap you misread."

Without looking again at the paper, she said, "I can read, you know. It says Chodstone House. Do you know where it is?"

"But... Please, the name of your guardian?"

She gazed again at the paper, hoping he couldn't tell she didn't know her own guardian's name. To cover up her reading of the name, she pushed the note under his magnificent nose. "James Porter, fourth Duke of Chodstone."

He had to lean back to read the script. His eyes, his mouth, his whole body tensed, and his aspect grew cold.

"Please step out of the carriage."

She scanned the area. Rows of townhouses lined the opposite side of the street to where they had stopped. She turned her head to gaze out of the other window. Nothing but scattered trees. She supposed that was a park where the gentry went to see and be seen, either walking—strolling more like—or driving in open carriages. "Are we here, then?"

He held out his hand to help her down but didn't answer. Instead, he flicked his hand at the driver. "Wait here."

"Aye, m'lord."

Once away from the carriage, Edward clasped Elizabeth's arm. "Why are you here?"

"Ouch, you're hurting me."

She tried to twist out of his clasp, certain that in polite society, men weren't supposed to touch women. Well, not highborn women anyway, and she was supposed to appear highborn. Had he seen through her disguise? He obviously thought nothing of touching her, and she knew he wouldn't do that to a true lady.

He glared at his hand and, as if he'd been burnt, quickly withdrew it. He asked with a tone similar but not quite the same as his earlier concerned timbre, "Who are you?"

She felt the color rise in her cheeks at his rudeness. "Why do you think I'm lying? Who the blazes are you?"

He blanched at her words.

Oops. Way to go at being highborn. She could have smacked herself. That wasn't even the worst curse she could come up with. These weren't people who were used to or had even heard some of the language that had the tendency to fall out of her mouth when she was angry.

She tried to look ashamed of her words.

"I'm sorry. I forgot English people are over-sensitive when it comes to... risqué—is that the right word?—speech. Anyway, I don't even want to know who you are, but I've already told you, I'm Elizabeth Davis, and if you could point me to Chodstone House, Manchester Square, I'd be much obliged."

Humor sparked in his intensely curious eyes and his mouth spread in a slow smile as he grazed his eyes down the front of her.

Uh oh, she would have to be more careful. He definitely wondered at her speech.

"It is right there." He pointed across the road to a great house.

She tipped her head back to take in the magnificent white structure. It was built on three levels and, going by the number of windows, had many rooms. A large portico covered the driveway, which bordered well-maintained gardens on either side of the house. The duke must have been extremely wealthy to have a separate townhouse.

Wow.

Izzy hurried to the entrance and the man's footfalls followed. Before she reached the steps, the twin black doors framed by two columns opened. What must have been a butler stood in the opening. He wore black trousers, an even blacker coat and vest over a white shirt and black tie, and ultra-clean white gloves. So shiny were his shoes, she could almost see her reflection in them.

His face was a closed book but his gaze, quizzical.

Scrunching the paper up in her hand once more, Izzy let out a huff of impatience and strode to the steps. There were only three, but she wasn't used to wearing long skirts, and she tripped on the first riser. The man behind her moved quickly to stop her from falling. He grasped her waist with his giant hands and held her.

She gasped, stiffening. Although he held her away from his body, his hands radiated warmth where they touched her. Regaining her mind and her balance, she pushed him away and cast him a dart-throwing glare.

A tic beat a staccato rhythm along the line of his right jaw. He stepped back and glanced down at his front.

Izzy couldn't help smiling. "Not a smudge."

The corners of his mouth twitched as if he was holding back a smile.

The butler cleared his throat.

Her rescuer was the first to regain his senses. "Ah, Hampton. Good evening."

He knew the butler? Surely that must mean he knew the duke too.

The butler bowed to Edward. "My lord." Then again to Izzy.

"I'd like to see the duke, please."

"Please come in. I will tell His Grace he has a visitor."

Izzy smiled and turned to her rescuer. "I'm sorry I ruined your night but thank you for bringing me here safely."

He gave a deep bow. "My pleasure." And with that, he spun on his heels and strode to his waiting carriage.

Izzy sighed. For some reason she was sorry to see him go. What? She was usually the one who left when pushed or manipulated by her friends into meeting men. He knew the duke, so she might see him again. She gave herself a mental slap. She was here to research that era, not become enamored with a stranger, no matter how good-looking said stranger was.

Izzy entered what she hoped would be her temporary home and stopped in the grandest entrance she'd ever set foot in. Feeling like a small child, she stared in awe at the great vault of the painted ceiling. She craned her neck trying to take it all in: paintings of women, men, cupids, and horses. She grimaced at the beauty of it all and looking down at her muddy slippers, hoped the duke wouldn't send her away.

CHAPTER 4

Izzy stood in awe of two sweeping staircases with carved wooden rails and banisters leading up to a curved landing that overlooked the entrance. An enormous chandelier with many candle holders hung from the ceiling but only the lower candles were lit. Mismatched chairs—some, definitely uncomfortable—and small tables stood against the walls between double and single doorways on both sides of the entrance.

She whipped her gaze around the paintings on the walls and up the staircases. It would take her a month of Sundays to look at all of them.

"Miss?"

She swung around. "I'm sorry, I thought you'd gone."

The butler frowned and looked a little confused. "Shouldn't your gentleman friend stay?"

"Oh, no, he's not a friend, he just gave me a lift here. As I said, I'm here to see the duke."

He glanced out of the still-open door and back at Izzy, his frown bringing his brows together. Tipping his head in a slight bow, he turned his back to her to close the door.

Izzy bit her bottom lip and wished she could see his face because she was sure that would tell her what his thoughts were.

A man wearing perfectly tailored evening wear—dark blue coat, an expertly folded white cravat, and black trousers—strode into the foyer. Izzy guessed he was in his mid-forties, maybe touching on fifty. It was hard to tell in the subdued lighting.

His gaze washed over Izzy and he smiled.

"I hope you don't mind me coming here but I... um... I am Mark and Dianne Davis's daughter."

His eyes widened. "Ah, I was wondering when I would meet you. Hampton, please bring tea." He raised his brows to Izzy. "Unless you would prefer to change first?"

"I don't have anything to change into."

"The maids will look after that but first I would like to talk."

"Of course."

He placed Izzy's hand on his arm and walked her into the room he'd emerged from earlier.

Izzy's mouth fell open at the splendor of the long front room, the pure luxury of the furnishings. The room was decorated as one would suspect—in chaises, settees, and spindly legged chairs of the time.

She ogled a grand tapestry featuring horses, dogs, and riders in red coats above the massive fireplace.

He cleared his throat and Izzy faced him.

He smiled. "Elizabeth?"

"How do you know?"

"You are fair-headed. Maxine is dark, Abigail's hair is reddish brown, and Garrett is a male."

She hesitated, but when he widened his smile and his eyes softened with crinkly laugh lines, she immediately went to him and hugged him.

He laughed.

Izzy quickly moved back. "I'm sorry, aren't I supposed to hug you?"

He chuckled and held out his arms. "Of course, you are. You are family."

His hold on her shoulders was fatherly and comfortable. He immediately felt like an old friend, someone she could trust. She smiled into his shoulder.

Once more apart, he said, "I'm so glad to see you again."

"You've met me before?"

"No, not in person, but I have seen pictures and have heard many wonderful stories about you all. It is as if I have known you for many years. Please sit down. Would you like a drink? Wine mayhap?"

"I'd love a glass of something red. Thanks." Deciding the gold embroidered settee was too good to sit on, she chose a smaller green chair near a small round table. She quickly seized a throw rug off the sofa and covered the chair before sitting down.

He handed her a small glass.

"Thank you, ah..." He was a duke, so Izzy was reasonably sure how to address him. "Your Grace."

The duke shook his head. "No, no. You will call me James when we're alone and we'll be such good friends."

He sat in the chair on the other side of the table. "The last picture I saw of you, you were ten and while you were a pretty thing then, you are beautiful now. Your parents must be so proud of you. So proud you had the courage to take such a long journey."

"They don't know I used the orb. They're... they had an accident and they're..."

A curious expression passed over his face. "Please don't fret, and remember, in my time, your parents aren't even born yet."

Izzy wiped the tears away. She hadn't thought of it like that, but now that he said it, it was somehow comforting that her parents still had their whole lives to live in the future.

Knowing eyes flickered in the subdued lighting. "The traveling, was it difficult?"

Izzy smiled to assure him. "Not really. Although, I don't think I'd like to make the habit of it my parents did."

The butler appeared at the door with a tray of tea and cakes. Chuckling at Izzy's last statement, James waved him in and began pouring the tea.

Izzy didn't much like tea but guessed she'd better get used to it. She accepted the cup and took a sip.

"Thank you, Hampton, that will be all," James said as he picked up his glass and sat down.

Hampton left and shut the door quietly behind him.

The duke questioned Izzy with a look. "Tell me, how old are you now? Three-and-twenty years?"

Izzy nodded, aware that was quite an age for a single woman in the early eighteen hundreds. She hoped Edward wouldn't judge her too old. *Huh? Where did that come from? And anyway, too old for what?* Tough bananas. He wasn't the pick of the crop, either.

Yes, he was.

"I've been expecting you," James said.

"You were expecting me? How? No one knew I was coming here."

"Your parents told me you would."

"How would they know that?"

"You would know that better than I. I know of your parents' travels, but not how they accomplished such great feats."

Izzy frowned trying to think how her parents knew she would go back to the nineteenth century.

"No matter, you are here now. I hope you like the countryside."

"The countryside? Why?"

"We leave for Chodstone Hall in three days."

Izzy tried not to let her disappointment show at not having the chance to see Edward again.

James must have mistaken her look because he said, "The country still has life. We will have balls and many entertainments. The season in London is all but finished until the New Year and I find Christmastide in the country more to my liking."

Izzy thought about the snowy sludge and mud and stench in the city. "It sounds lovely."

She stifled a yawn.

"You are tired. We can talk more on the morrow but right now, I'll have Hampton show you to your room."

ONCE IZZY WAS ALONE IN HER ROOM SHE SPUN AROUND slowly, trying to take in everything at once. A grand four-poster bed took pride and place against the back wall. The peacock-blue hangings were tied to the posts, giving the bed a tent-like effect. And the muted blues of the bedcovers and dark blue and white pillows had her looking forward to snuggling into them.

The opulence she could get used to, but as she ran her hand along the edge of the small writing desk, she knew in her heart she could never live with the lack of technology.

A small pile of loose paper and a fountain pen had her frowning. Not even a notebook. She was sure they had notebooks in 1811, and if they did, she hoped James would get them for her.

She smiled. She liked the Duke of Chodstone very much

and she silently thanked her parents for him. Once her parents came to mind, Izzy wondered how they had known she would travel to 1811 and how they had known she would stay with the duke?

Those questions would have to wait until she returned and spoke to Max and Garrett, but especially Bree. Their cousin knew more about all of it, and Izzy hoped that following her disappearance, Bree would have told Max and Garrett more.

No matter. For now, she intended to make the most of this crazy chance.

Bending over the writing desk, she tried the fountain pen. She wanted to write a detailed diary of everything she saw, felt, touched, and especially heard. She grinned, hoping the servants weren't opposed to sharing gossipy details with her.

Ink blobbed on the paper as soon as she touched the nib to it. She didn't mind writing longhand—it was a nice change from typing or dictating sometimes—but the pen was going to take some getting used to. She frowned. Ball-point pens wouldn't even be invented until late eighteen hundred. And while some Italian invented a writing machine of sorts for his blind sister in 1801, commercial machines wouldn't be around until eighteen-sixty-something.

She scratched out her name a few times, then wiped the pen with a cloth that she guessed had been placed there for just that purpose and rested it on the paper.

Three soft knocks sounded. She pushed the writing implements aside and opened the door to find a young woman about her age standing there.

The girl bobbed a small curtsy and said, "Good evening, Miss Davis. I am Lucy."

She stood there looking from the floor to Izzy, to over Izzy's shoulder into the room. Izzy followed her eyes and then questioned her with a look. She had the feeling she knew why the girl was there but wasn't completely certain.

Lucy said, "I am to be your abigail while you are in attendance at Chodstone House."

"My Abigail?" Izzy frowned, confused by the use of her sister's name. Realization slowly dawned. "Oh. Okay, come in then." She stepped aside so Lucy could pass.

The girl went straight to the dark wood wardrobe and, after a moment, chose what Izzy presumed was her nightgown and wrap. She draped them over the bed and began to move closer to Izzy than she was comfortable with. Izzy stepped back.

"I will draw you a bath immediately."

Although she tried to hide it, Izzy noted her top lip curling up. "Sorry about the smell. I had an accident," Izzy said.

Lucy's brows rose slightly but she didn't ask what kind of accident. Instead she said, "I'll help you out of your dress and once you have bathed, I'll help you into your night rail."

"No, that's okay. I can do it myself."

Lucy's brows drew closer for a second, but she stilled her expression again. "If you are certain."

"I am. Thanks, though."

The maid bobbed in a quick curtsy, and with an odd smile on her face, she quietly left the room.

Yawning, Izzy gazed at the bed and, reaching up behind her neck, began unbuttoning her dress. She could only go down so far, so she then stretched her hands behind her back instead, but the position was so awkward, she only managed to undo one more button.

Looking to the door, she let out a huff. How could she be so stupid? Max had helped her into the dumb dress, and she needed someone to help her out of it. She also needed to go to the bathroom. She scanned the room. *I hope there* is *a bathroom.*

Sighing, she opened the door. Lucy was standing there with a small but self-satisfied smile on her lips, which she quickly dropped at Izzy's frown.

"You knew I'd need you, didn't you?"

"Yes, Miss Davis."

Lucy stepped over the threshold and turned to face Izzy. "Although, I wasn't sure if you would decide to sleep in your day dress."

Izzy looked down at the street filth on her dress. "What? No. It's filthy."

Screwing up her nose, Lucy covered it with her hand. "And it does smell something awful, if you don't mind my saying so, Miss Davis."

Izzy laughed. "You're right there, and please do not call me Miss Davis. My name is Elizabeth, but I like Izzy."

The girl seemed to think about that for a minute. "That is very kind of you, Miss..."

Izzy frowned.

"...Izzy, but His Grace wouldn't like it."

"James won't care."

Lucy started at the mention of her employer's first name. The poor thing wasn't comfortable with the first name thing, and although Izzy liked being called 'my lady', James's employees must have been told how to address her. However, Miss Davis sounded too formal coming from her own maid— ah... *abigail.* "Okay, what about you call me 'Izzy' when we're alone and 'miss' when we're not?"

She smiled. "Thank you, yes, that would do well."

"Good. Now get me out of this thing."

Once Izzy had washed and dressed, she couldn't wait to get into bed. Lucy put more wood on the fire, and the warm glow made Izzy even sleepier. As soon as she closed her eyes, her rescuer appeared. His dark eyes melted her insides and she smiled as she drifted off to sleep.

The next day passed in a flurry of activity. Izzy's mind was in a whirl. James had employed a modiste to bring the latest fashions to the house and furnish Izzy with a small wardrobe. He said they would have more made to order at Chodstone Hall, but he wanted her to have a beautiful gown for the ball they were to attend the following night.

After the last fitting, Izzy stood in front of the long mirror. The blue in her wide eyes matched the material of the gown perfectly. How could they have known? James said the modiste had made the gown for another client, but the lady had refused to accept it, saying it was ugly.

Her loss, thought Izzy as she regarded her reflection.

CHAPTER 5

After a day at the races, Edward was looking forward to a quiet dinner alone with his mother. It seemed no matter where he went, other mothers were everywhere, dragging along their daughters, lying in wait for him. He couldn't understand his short-tempered impatience with the women. He usually enjoyed the attentions of so many beautiful women, some of whom would do anything to have his name on their friendship list.

The widows were the most welcoming. As a male, he had to forgive his father's weak tendencies where women were concerned. There were plenty on offer out there. As a son, he would never forgive his father's slights against his mother, who endured his endless affairs, some of which were the talk of the *ton*, for years.

The late Earl of Wellsneath may not have been the best husband or father, but, in the early years, he succeeded in making his estates prosper. Later in life he lost all interest in everything, preferring to spend his time in gaming hells or with his mistresses.

Edward, however, was determined not to follow in his father's footsteps and, as much fun as Edward's social life had once afforded him, the responsibility of his family now rested firmly on his shoulders. He was the Earl of Wellsneath, and it was up to him to build up the prosperity of his family's holdings and look after the tenants who worked them.

Edward had lived and worked with his tenants for the last year. He enjoyed talking with them and listening to their ideas. He also had plans of his own that he was keen to implement.

He loved the time he spent in the country. The people were friendly, much friendlier than those in the city, and there was more to do than sit around at White's or endure the endless vacuous entertainments offered by society.

Fishing and hunting were high priorities, but managing the estates took up much of his time and he found he enjoyed the work. This astounded him, his friends, and his mother, the dowager countess. Perhaps that was more to do with his prank-filled university days than his intelligence, he mused with a self-deprecating humor.

The only thing that suited him in the city was when Parliament was in session. Engagement in politics was also a surprise enjoyment, and he would not take his role lightly. The reduction of taxes was his main aim once Parliament sat next.

Once his valet, Trapem, had finished laying out his clothes, he began shaving Edward's facial stubble. If Edward had his way, he would never shave again, but an earl had to present himself in an estimable manner.

"I hope your day proved pleasant, my lord."

"I'm just glad the London season is over, and many have already begun to make the pilgrimage to their country estates for Christmastide."

Edward frowned. When had he decided not to go to

Halting Castle for Christmastide? He didn't know when or even why for that matter. The affections of the women of the *ton* had become annoying at best, excruciatingly boring at worst, so why was he now staying in London?

Once suitably attired, Edward joined his mother in the parlor. She was sitting on the settee close to the fire. It being only the second night she had worn colors in a year, Edward scowled at her puffy-sleeved, yellow gown. He had thought she would ease into colors; mayhap navy, or some other dark color would have been more suitable for the first sennight or two.

He schooled his face when his mother turned to him.

"Ah, Edward, I have been meaning to talk with you."

He sat in the armchair on her right and accepted a glass of sherry.

She eyed him as if choosing an exquisite jewel.

He didn't like that look and knew what she would say next. It was always the same. Make a suitable match, produce an heir and a spare. Not that she would say 'a spare' but the meaning was unmistakable. After all, that is what she had done, and Edward was the spare.

She put her teacup down. "Christmastide is upon us, and I have accepted invitations to only the best entertainments. Only the highest-born new and existing debutantes will be in attendance. Lady Todfrey's ball is tomorrow night, and you need to make a good match now that you have accepted your role in life. Have your thoughts centered on anyone in particular?"

He hated being a prize to be won by the most heavily dowered daughter of titled gentry. Elizabeth's face floated across his mind. "What can you tell me about Chodstone's ward?"

Surprise and confusion flashed across his mother's

features but she quickly displaced them with her formal look. "Ward? Chodstone has no ward."

"She is living with him as we speak."

His mother thought about that for a moment. "She must have lost her parents recently and has just now became his ward." Her face brightened. "How delightful for him."

Edward knew his mother, knew she was itching to speak to Chodstone and find out the truth before the gossipers took hold. For some reason, she had a soft spot for the duke.

Changing the subject, she said, "Lady Crompton will be joining us for dinner."

"Lady Crompton?"

He might not have been inclined to anyone in particular, but he knew his mother favored the woman. After all, Vera was the daughter of a wealthy merchant and she was also a wealthy baron's widow. Her large dowry was well known, and even he had to admit she was beautiful—so much so, that in her coming out year, she was acclaimed that season's Incomparable.

As if Edward's thinking about her conjured her presence, the butler announced Lady Crompton's arrival.

Edward and Alice stood at the same time and Edward bowed as she stepped over the threshold into the drawing room.

Vera dipped in a curtsy. Her perfect coiffure embodied the latest fashion: ebony hair braided in a complicated knot on top of her head with thin ringlets falling over one shoulder. The sapphire-blue gown fell from a high waist to just above her blue slippers. She was the picture of perfection, but something about her had thwarted his interest.

The moment Vera smiled, Edward realized then, that was one reason. Her smiles never lit her eyes, eyes that always calculated if the person she was meeting with deserved her attention. An image of a set of blue eyes flashing confusion, anger, worry, laughter, and defiance in quick succession emerged in Edward's mind.

A silent chuckle grew in his mind at the thought of the lost beauty whose eyes had shone the moment she smiled—pure and natural.

He suspected no other smile would compete with his memory. He wanted—needed—to see Elizabeth again. He told himself it was so the reality would dispel whatever romantic exaggeration his mind had made of the lost chit.

❖

To even the numbers, Alice had invited Edward's longtime friend and school cohort, Mr Oliver Marshal.

Over the meal, his mother talked about her day. As she spoke, Edward looked at her as he'd never looked at her before. He was a little surprised to see she was still attractive and hadn't gone to fat as many matrons did as they approached their fifties.

Her fair hair hadn't yet begun to turn gray and her green eyes still held a hint of gaiety. With a start, he realized that twinkle of life had only appeared following his father's funeral.

Of course, he knew she'd endured a troubled marriage, though he never liked to think on it. She had been miserable from the moment her bedridden father assigned her to marry the then Earl of Wellsneath. The old earl needed an heir and Alice's father needed to make a suitable match for his daughter. The old earl had sought Alice out and to Edward's thinking, had pressured his grandfather on his deathbed.

And Edward had heard the gossip about the man who was his father. A rogue and wastrel. A gambler and rake.

His mother raised her eyebrows in question. He hadn't

meant to stare. He smiled in response and quickly focused on his plate.

How old was she exactly? He knew she had married young—seventeen—and she birthed Thomas a year later at eighteen, then himself when she was nineteen. He was eight-and-twenty, so that would make her seven-and-forty. Not so old as he had thought.

For some unexplained reason his encounter with the lost beauty, the Lady Elizabeth, filled his mind. He frowned. He had assumed she was a lady, but that was before he knew she was an American. So probably not a daughter of a titled English gentleman. Mayhap an American heiress.

While Elizabeth was young, she wasn't as young as his mother had been when she'd married. Elizabeth... why he thought of her on first-name terms he couldn't fathom. He had never before had the urge to address a young woman, especially an innocent, by her first name. He decided to keep a check on his thoughts in case they fell from his tongue without his knowledge.

Miss Davis, Miss Davis, Miss Davis.

Again, an image of her, disheveled and with wide, curious, though confused eyes appeared in his mind. She had a strange wisdom about her despite her apparent unworldliness. Would she age gracefully as his mother had? He expected so.

Vera's voice intruded on his thoughts. Had she just mentioned Miss Davis?

Edward started. "Miss Davis?"

His mother, Vera, and Marshal all stared at him.

Leaning over the table, Vera's eyes sparkled with malice. "The Duke of Chodstone has taken on a fiancée."

"What?" Both Edward and his mother asked at the same time.

"The *on-dit* has it, Chodstone has taken in a Miss Elizabeth Davis. He says she is his ward, but the *haut ton* suspect her to be his fiancée. Lady Gambol said as much at the opera this afternoon."

"How could Lady Gambol come by that information?"

"Her lady's maid is affianced with a footman in the duke's employ." She waved her hand about. "You know how servants gossip."

"I don't believe it," Alice said.

Edward stopped listening to their conversation and went silent again. His mind was awhirl. Was that what had made him suspicious of Elizabeth turning up alone in the middle of the night? When she had said Chodstone was her guardian, something about the flinch in her eyes told Edward she wasn't quite telling the truth. Had Chodstone taken on an American heiress?

"Wellsneath."

He started and again his mother and their guests were staring at him.

His mother raised her brows. "Are you even listening to me?"

"I apologize. I meant no disrespect. I was thinking about a conversation I had with a friend." Could he honestly call Miss Davis his friend? He had only met her the night before and they hadn't even been formally introduced. He quickly turned his thoughts to another conversation he had earlier that day.

His mother sat back and regarded Edward with a knowing aspect only mothers could use. "It must have been a fascinating conversation indeed. Can you tell me what this conversation was about?"

"We were discussing the notion of growing grapes."

She tilted her head, encouraging him to go on.

"Ah, so it's Bledstone you've been talking with?" Oliver Marshal asked.

Despite a gallant attempt to appear interested, Vera

43

couldn't hide her bored look. She didn't like business being discussed at meal times. Or any other time, Edward thought. Neither did she like politics. The plight of others meant nothing to her. He silently snorted. Unless it was the latest *ton* gossip, or the latest French fashions, she wasn't much interested.

"Yes. He is keen to make wine, or at least to sell to the wineries that have begun to appear throughout England now that French wine is so expensive."

Alice clapped her hands. "I think it's a marvelous idea, and do you know Chodstone has also planted acres of vines?"

Edward frowned. He hadn't known. What he did know, though, was his father hated the Duke of Chodstone and had warned Edward at every chance to have nothing to do with the man. His father had called Chodstone a wastrel of the worst account. Edward smiled at that. One wastrel would know another.

"You could ask him for advice, mayhap?"

"That won't be necessary. Bledstone has all the experience I need."

The Duke of Chodstone was the last person he would go to for advice.

Vera asked, "Will you be traveling to Halting Castle for Christmastide?"

Edward's beef-laden fork hung in midair between his plate and his mouth. "No." Miss Davis's image once again filled his mind. "Not this year."

A smile lit his mother's lips. "I am so pleased. I am leaving for Wellsneath in a few days and you can accompany me. We will have a lovely, quiet, family Christmastide."

Edward drew his brows together in irritation. *Leave London? Now?* "I'd like to stay here for a time. Mayhap take a trip to Bledstone's estate."

"But you know how I hate to travel alone."

"You won't be alone, Mother. You will have your abigail, the footmen, and the driver at your beck and call."

Vera very daintily touched her serviette to the corners of her mouth, one at a time. Edward could almost hear her mind working. She smiled at Edward. She was pleased he would be staying on in London. He hoped she didn't think it was because of her.

His mother gave an impatient wave of her hand. "That's not the same and you know it. You have never wanted to stay in London at Christmastide before, and if you're not going on to Halting Castle, why can't you come to Wellsneath with me? I want you with me."

She popped a bitesize piece of potato in her mouth and chewed it as if the tiny morsel were at fault for her disappointment.

It was true, Edward loved spending time at Wellsneath. The people, the hunting. However, he could not for the life of him get Elizabeth—uh, how he loved that name...no, Miss Davis—out of his mind. He needed to meet her again to see if the darkness of the night they met had messed with his senses. She couldn't possibly be the vision he imagined her to be. Her touch couldn't possibly send razor shards straight to his stomach. And he had to find out if she was affianced to the duke in truth. Surely, Chodstone was too old for her.

He glanced at his mother.

Age wasn't a deterrent to a good match, at least from the husband's point of view. His father could attest to that. Mayhap their young wives thought differently.

Edward also had the strangest notion: Miss Elizabeth Davis wasn't who she said she was. Had Chodstone really a ward? If so, why hadn't anyone ever heard of her before? His mother hadn't even known about her. And while she dismissed Chodstone's engagement out of hand, wouldn't she have known if he had a ward?

He smiled, trying to comfort his mother. "I will write."

"Oh, yes." She pushed her plate away. "Letters will keep me company."

He wondered why she seemed so intent on him accompanying her. "You will have your friends to keep you company whenever you feel the need, of that I am certain."

The dowager countess's green eyes flashed, then just as quickly softened in understanding. "You have other business in London, I think." She glanced at Vera, who had suddenly become intrigued with the conversation.

Edward's mouth tightened at her smug aspect, but he couldn't help his lips twitching in a smile. His mother was right. There was someone he wanted to meet again, but that someone wasn't Vera.

How did his mother know him so well, considering his father had gone out of his way to keep him and his brother apart from their mother? His father thought mothers mollycoddled their sons to such an extent that the boys would never become real men as the earl himself had.

Edward gave a small non-committal shrug.

Alice took that as a yes. "I had begun to worry you would never find anyone suitable." She tilted her head the way she did when in a quandary. "I do hope she is suitable society. Your countess has to be."

"Please, Mother, no lectures. I am aware of the role I play in society. You need not concern yourself; there will be no scandal."

She seemed fine with that and stood up. Vera, Edward, and Oliver also got to their feet.

"Then we will leave you to contemplate your future." She curtsied. "Thank you for your company, Mr Marshal."

Oliver bowed. "Thank you, my lady."

Vera dutifully followed Alice to the parlor. Edward knew his mother would encourage the woman, but he couldn't do anything about that. He just had to make certain he didn't attend any events where Vera would be in attendance. An impossible task.

"Brandy, Marshal?"

Oliver Marshal smiled. "For certain, and then you can tell me what that dance was all about."

CHAPTER 6

The next night Edward tried to slip into the Todfrey ball unnoticed, but his mother must have kept her eyes on the door the entire night, because she was already moving quickly in his direction. She held herself well, but Edward knew by the way she scooped the hem of her peach satin gown just over her slippers, she was hurrying as elegantly as possible to his side.

Her hair, still shiny blonde, and her figure belied a woman of seven-and-forty. He was proud she was his mother—not just because of her appearance, but because she was also the most compassionate woman he had ever known. She was kind to everyone and spent many an hour with her many charities, some of which she trapped him into helping with. Not that he minded but he liked to let her think he did.

He gave her a deep bow and came up smiling, that he hoped she would take as a true effort on his part.

"You're late."

"I apologize. I was discussing some business with Chalms."

"What is the estate manager doing in town?"

Edward opened his mouth to answer, but she kept talking. "Never mind that now. Vera has not left the dance floor. She has many beaus lined up and they all appear to be smitten with her."

Wondering if the men really had high thoughts of Vera, or if they thought a widow was willing prey, Edward scanned the room. As at all such events, he found it hard to differentiate one from the other. The décor of stately homes these days was all much the same: some pastel or other, this one was blue, covered the walls, that were littered with paintings of landscapes and foxhunts. Uncomfortable chairs and very few comfortable settees circled what had become a dance floor, and trestle tables abounded with plates of food, champagne bottles and glasses, and of course, lemonade.

Why they couldn't serve whiskey was beyond him.

Footmen were pressed into service as waiters and, carrying round trays laden with glasses of champagne, they ducked and weaved around the throng of ladies and gentlemen all dressed in the latest fashion. Some guests were more suited to the modern fashions than others.

He spied the Marquess of Todfrey across the room talking to the Duke of Chodstone. While Chodstone, as usual, was scrupulously fitted out, Todfrey could very well do with a tailor who knew how to use a measuring tape. His waistcoat appeared to be a size or two too small, and Edward worried his buttons would pop if he kept laughing at whatever Chodstone had said to him.

Chodstone sported an understated attire: a white shirt, black waistcoat with matching coat, and an impeccably crafted white cravat.

"Chodstone's here," Edward said flatly.

"Why should he not be? Few of the *ton* would decline an invitation from the Marchioness of Todfrey. To insult her would be paramount to reputation suicide."

He doubted the Duke of Chodstone would ever suffer a taint on his reputation. He was far too wealthy and, with the ear of the Prince Regent, too powerful for even the likes of the Marchioness of Todfrey. The *haut* of the *ton* bowed and scraped to him as if he were of true royal blood. The duke could do no wrong in their eyes. That, Edward knew for a certainty.

Edward's eyes wandered in search of Chodstone's ward. He found her in a small group of ladies, which included Lady Glastbury.

Elizabeth was breathtaking in a blue gown that matched the azure of her eyes perfectly. The neckline was chaste, but her curves could not be hidden.

She seemed out of sorts. The astonished look she gave Lady Glastbury had him smiling. Mayhap the woman was being her usual self, sharing malicious gossip about all and sundry.

Lady Glastbury smiled over Elizabeth's head and Edward followed her gaze to Vera, who raised her brows and returned a thin smile. Vera wore a green gown. She had apparently seen the same modiste as the Dowager Countess of Glastbury, because the neckline of her gown was as low as the piece the countess wore.

Lady Glastbury was always pushing the lines of decency, and it would seem Vera was the perfect apprentice.

His mother tapped him on the arm with her fan. "I hope you will ask Vera to dance."

He dipped his head but said, "Have you met Chodstone's ward?"

"I have and I fear Vera has the wrong of it. Miss Davis is much too young and innocent to be anything other than his ward, and I think he will make a grand guardian. He is, after all, a gentleman of the highest order."

"Is she nice?"

"Nice?" His mother gave him a confused look. "Of course she is nice—didn't I just say so? And I am so glad she was able to make use of the gown Vera didn't like."

Edward glanced at Elizabeth. The gown conformed to her shape perfectly. The style would never have suited Vera's tall form.

Noting Chodstone dip his head toward them, Edward turned his scowling face to his mother.

She smiled at Chodstone but tapped her fan on Edward's arm again. "Don't scowl like that, you look like your father."

"I don't like that man."

"Who? Your father?"

"Chodstone."

"Now you sound like your father."

She tried to make her tone light, but Edward knew she worried that he would become like his father. And while he understood her marriage wasn't anything she would have wished for, he had loved his father and thought him a fine parent.

It wasn't until after his father's death that Edward learned the extent of his rapscallion ways.

Chodstone made his way through the throng toward Edward and his mother. On the way he paused to speak to Elizabeth. Her eyes lit up and her smile sent a bolt of joy through Edward. After dipping into curtsies to her companions, she joined Chodstone.

Edward's mother gave his arm another quick flick of her fan. "Be nice."

Taking Lady Wellsneath's hand, Chodstone bowed low from the waist, brushing his lips over the back of her hand as he did so. "Lady Wellsneath."

"Your Grace, how good it is to see you again."

A small grunt of irritation passed Edward's lips.

Standing once more, Chodstone dipped his head to Edward. "Wellsneath."

Edward mirrored his movements. "Chodstone."

"Please let me introduce my ward, Miss Elizabeth Davis. Miss Davis this is Al—ah...Lady Wellsneath and her son, the Earl of Wellsneath."

She bent her head and curtsied. The moment she straightened, Edward took her hand and bowed over it, his lips hovering just above her glove. "I am glad we have been formally introduced."

She glanced to Chodstone. "Yes, yes we have. Thank you."

The duke held his hand out to Edward's mother. "May I have the honor of this dance?"

Alice beamed. "Of course." She tapped her fan on Edward's arm. "Wellsneath, introduce Miss Davis to some ladies of her age."

She didn't wait for his agreement before taking to the dance floor.

Edward knew he was scowling like a spoiled boy at his mother's separation from him, but he couldn't help it. He hated the way Chodstone sought his mother, especially since she'd come out of mourning.

He silently slapped himself. How could he be so selfish? The poor woman had been in mourning for two years: first with Thomas's unexpected death and then with her husband's demise.

Hoping she would find more suitable dance partners, Edward turned to Elizabeth. "It seems you have found your city legs."

"I have. Why didn't you tell them you saved me that night and took me to the duke's house?"

"We hadn't been formally introduced, and without being so, it was not the thing to talk about."

"I see."

She said the words, but Edward was certain she didn't see, not at all. He cleared his throat.

"Would you like some refreshment?"

"I would love some."

He offered his forearm, and after a slight hesitation she placed her hand on his arm and he led her to the table.

As they drank lemonade, Edward heard Oliver's voice. He turned just in time to hear Roger Harmer say, "The marriage mart isn't the place to find love."

Edward smiled at that. Roger hadn't found his love in the marriage mart. He'd found Lady Henrietta in his carriage, of all places.

"I have to agree with Harmer," Edward said.

Oliver grinned. "Good to see you again, Wellsneath." He shook Edward's hand heartily.

Harmer plucked two glasses of lemonade from the table and, grinning at both men, hurried toward his red-haired wife.

Oliver let out a grunt. "You might agree with Harmer, but nonetheless you are here."

"Yes, I am here under Mother's orders."

Oliver stared at Elizabeth. Edward couldn't blame the man. She was stunning—easily the most beautiful woman at the ball.

"I see," Oliver said.

Edward chuckled. "Not that kind of order. Please, let me introduce Miss Elizabeth Davis. She is visiting from the Americas. Miss Elizabeth, this is an old friend of mine, Mr Marshal."

Elizabeth seemed to hesitate for a second, then curtsied.

Oliver bowed. "Pleased to make your acquaintance, Miss Elizabeth. Are you guesting at the Wellsneaths?"

"No, I am the ward of the Duke of Chodstone."

Oliver raised his brows at Edward and Edward tried to

force the heat out of his cheeks. He'd told Oliver about his first meeting with the young woman and how she was either the ward of the duke or, if they were to believe Lady Crompton, Chodstone's affianced. However, he hadn't mentioned Elizabeth's name.

"Yes, it was quite a surprise."

Edward expected Oliver to be more curious about the beautiful American, but his friend's mind appeared to be elsewhere. He followed Oliver's gaze.

"Ah, Aubrey is here," Oliver said. "I hear Percy died." He shook his head in sympathy. "Most unfortunate."

Oliver pressed his lips together, but the corners of his mouth rose in a smile.

Edward laughed. "Aubrey still hasn't forgiven him, I'm afraid."

Poor Aubrey had been looking forward to continuing the freedom of life he'd had as a second son. He had already made connections in Scotland Yard and fancied himself a detective of the finest form. However, now Aubrey had to take on the duties of the Viscount Grisham.

Izzy wondered if she should have curtsied to a mister. She grimaced. Oh, so much to learn. Though she did like the fact that Edward didn't only have titled friends.

She liked Edward's friends and enjoyed listening to their playful teasing of one another. She had a hunch, though, that Oliver Marshal wanted to be some place else. His eyes kept glancing in the direction of two beautiful women. Izzy zeroed in on the one he couldn't take his eyes off. She was gorgeous, with her glossy dark hair and pretty ringlets falling over her shoulder. Her large brown eyes met Oliver's gaze time after time. Oh, they had it bad. She wondered if they knew one another but something about the woman's shy glances told Izzy they didn't.

"Ah, Lord Wellsneath?" she said, hoping it was okay for her to interrupt their conversation.

He pierced her with his dark gaze. "Yes?"

"Ah." *Oh, come on Izzy, get the words out and stop looking at the man.* "I was wondering if I might be introduced to some women." She pointed with her fan. "Like those ones there."

"Of course, the Ladies Edgehill are well known in London, and they would be suitable companions for the ward of a duke." He turned to Oliver. "If I may be so presumptuous?"

"Yes, but I must tell you, I have not been introduced to them as yet, although it seems Grisham has their ear."

The way Mr Marshal's face darkened at the mention of his friend's name had Izzy wondering if they were both enamored with the same woman.

Edward and Elizabeth followed Oliver to the women. She loved the way he placed her hand on his forearm. It was both civilized and provocative at the same time.

By the time they arrived, the redhead was dancing, and by the way Lord Grisham was staring at her and her dance partner, Izzy guessed he had his sights set on her and not the brunette after all.

Lord Wellsneath cleared his throat as they arrived at the small party and Izzy hid her smile behind her fan. The dark-haired girl blushed up a storm at Wellsneath's wide smile. How Izzy felt for the poor girl. Izzy blushed at Edward's every glance also.

"Would you care to introduce us to your friends, Lord Grisham?"

"Pardon?" Lord Grisham's eyes widened as he turned away from the dancers. He grabbed Edward's hand and shook it. "Wellsneath!"

They talked a bit about Lord Grisham becoming a viscount and Edward, an earl, and Edward promised to meet him the first day Parliament sat, to give him the lay of the land.

While they talked, Izzy gave a big friendly smile to the young woman who had caught Oliver Marshal's eye.

Edward must have seen Izzy, because he said, "I do apologize for my deplorable manners. Please, let me introduce Miss Elizabeth Davis, ward of the Duke of Chodstone."

Lord Grisham bowed to Izzy, who bobbed in a quick curtsy. With the number of times she had to curtsy, Izzy decided she could do away with squats in her morning exercise regime.

"And please," Lord Grisham said. "Let me introduce Lady Jane Edgehill, eldest daughter of the late Earl of Glastbury."

The dark-haired woman curtsied, and Izzy did the same.

Lord Grisham continued with the introductions. "Lady Edgehill, these are my friends, Lord Wellsneath and Mr Oliver Marshal."

Lady Edgehill smiled as she curtsied to Edward. "Lord Wellsneath and I have met." She had to half turn to curtsy to Mr Marshal, and Izzy was impressed with her sense of balance.

"Mr Marshal," Lady Edgehill said with a shy smile.

Mr Marshal bowed over her hand and brushed his lips on her glove. Izzy wondered if that wasn't a little too risqué for that time.

He straightened and gave the girl a sexy smile. Goodness, Izzy thought. If she hadn't already met Edward, she would be swooning at the man's feet. The three of them—Edward, Oliver, and Aubrey—must be the most eligible bachelors in all of society.

"Is the duke here?" Jane asked.

"Yes." Edward looked about and his eyes narrowed on the dance floor. "He's dancing with Lady Wellsneath at present."

Izzy wondered why Edward resented the duke so much but directed her words to Jane. "So pleased to meet someone my own age."

Jane smiled. "This must be quite a bit different from your America."

Izzy laughed. "Oh yes, quite different than my America." *If you only knew*, she thought.

The strains of a waltz filled the room. Edward bowed to Izzy. "Would you care to dance?"

"Sure, but I must warn you, I'm not a great dancer." *At least not these sorts of dances.*

He looked at Izzy as if she had two heads. Now what had she said wrong?

He said, "Just follow me."

She shrugged. "Lead the way, my lord." She twisted her head back to Jane. "I hope we'll meet again soon."

Jane's brows rose but she smiled widely. "I do hope so."

Izzy laughed inwardly at the way Edward held her at arm's length. She followed him as well as she could, trying to keep her feet away from his so she wouldn't step on his highly polished boots. It didn't take her long to start getting the hang of the dance, but she wished she could be closer to him. The way he held her was so sterile, she couldn't relax into the music.

He must have thought so too, because as they turned, he pulled her in closer. She smiled; her gaze riveted on his perfectly tied cravat. That was better but there was still ample room between them. At least she could follow him, and as the dance progressed, they became as one, waltzing around the room as if no one else existed.

Though they were quite a distance apart, Izzy noted their bodies were still closer than the other dancers'. Warmth spread across her back under his hand, and she let the music wash over her as she breathed in his spicy scent. Was that cinnamon she smelt? Nice.

"Are you enjoying the night?"

Izzy frowned. Why did he have to go and spoil it? She tipped her head back. "I am. Thank you."

The music finished. "Mother is waving for us to join her."

He crooked his arm and Izzy immediately placed her hand on his forearm, liking the tradition very much.

"My lady, Chodstone," Edward said, when they arrived.

"Miss Elizabeth," the duke said. "I fear we must depart. I have an early appointment on the morrow."

"Oh, so soon." She gazed at Edward. "I was hoping to dance some more."

The duke cleared his throat and whispered in her ear. "You cannot dance more than one dance with Wellsneath."

Darn, she had forgotten that rule. "Of course, yes, it is getting late, isn't it?"

Edward bowed. "Perhaps another time?"

Izzy curtsied. "Perhaps."

As the duke retrieved their coats, Lady Vera Crompton paused beside Izzy.

"Miss Davis, are you leaving so soon?"

"Yes."

She eyed Izzy from head to foot with a pinched expression. "I see the modiste found another customer for the gown I refused delivery of."

Izzy looked down at her gown. *Why did it have to be her?* "She said you didn't like it."

"I abhorred it. Of all the shades of blue in the world, why she would choose that one, I could not fathom. I specifically said the color of the sea."

Izzy always thought the sea looked more green than blue.

Perhaps that was what confused the modiste. "I love the color."

"I also chose the latest fashion plate from France and," she glared at the dress, "that style is not what I asked for. It is so last season." She looked over the ballroom. "See? Not another puffed sleeve to be seen or such a high neckline. Even the matrons' gowns are more fashionable than that."

Heat burned Izzy's cheeks. She scanned the other women and could see no puffed sleeves or high necklines. If she'd known the latest fashion, she could have asked the modiste to fix it, but not knowing was her problem. She would have to become more conversant with what the latest fashions were if she was to make a good impression in society.

Suddenly Izzy couldn't get out of the house quickly enough.

CHAPTER 7

After reluctantly leaving Elizabeth with Chodstone, Edward wandered with his mother around the stuffy ballroom. A picture of the beautiful American with full, pouting lips wouldn't leave him. It was clear to Edward she was disappointed about having to leave, and he wanted to believe it was because she was enjoying his company.

The American was making him feel out of sorts, so much so that his ire rose when Chodstone whispered in her shell-like ear. What had he said that changed her mind so quickly about leaving the ball?

The duke and Elizabeth seemed strangely close for two people who'd met only a few nights before. Something wasn't right about their relationship, and he intended to find out what it was.

The ballroom was stuffy and if he couldn't spend any more time with Elizabeth, Edward just wanted to go home.

His mother stopped suddenly. "I need to talk with my friend. Why don't you ask Vera to dance?"

He gave an exasperated sigh to show his mother his annoyance but acquiesced anyway.

Making his way through the crowd and dodging the mothers dragging their daughters toward him, Edward came face to face with Vera.

He swept low in a bow. "Lady Crompton, you look lovely tonight."

She smiled. "Thank you, my lord."

Edward tipped his head to Vera's companion. "As do you, Lady Glastbury."

Under his regard, Lady Glastbury let out a laugh and blushed like a debutante in her first season.

Edward turned to Vera. "Lady Crompton. Would you care to dance?"

A smile spread along Vera's lips in a slow, seductive way he'd seen her offer many a gentleman. He held out his arm and she threaded her arm in his. Instead of letting him lead her to the dance floor, she led him.

A thought crossed his mind, a marriage to Vera would mean she would always be leading him here or there—would probably take over his life and house. He shuddered at the thought of always trying to find comfort away from home. He liked his home in London and especially valued the warmth and freedom of Wellsneath Manor.

She threw smiles to everyone they passed, obviously enjoying society's attention. Mayhap she'd prefer to stay in London when he ventured to his country home.

Thank goodness, the dance was a quadrille and not a waltz. He had to admit he enjoyed the waltz with Elizabeth, relishing the feel of her in his arms. He delighted in her fresh, untrammeled beauty, the scent of flowers in her hair, and her quick smiles.

The last time he had waltzed with Vera, she very nearly became the latest *on-dit* with the way she tried to press in closer to him. Thankfully, he was stronger than she and was able to keep her at the proper distance.

However, the duke's ward was another thing entirely. The desire to pull her even closer had all but overwhelmed him when they danced.

He set his jaw and schooled his features. He had to break whatever spell the American had him under before *he* did something scandalous.

On the dance floor, the thought crossed his mind that no other woman fit so perfectly in his arms as Elizabeth.

Vera grimaced as the music began. Had she been expecting a waltz? By the glare she gave the musicians, Edward suspected she had. Viscount Harvey Blaxtor moved away from the pianist. Had he asked the musicians to change the set order?

Blaxtor flicked his brown hair back from his forehead and gave a slight tip of his head to Edward as they took their places on the dance floor. He was partnered with a blushing young debutante.

As the couples moved apart, Blaxtor leaned toward Edward, and whispered. "Her mama thought a waltz was to be had, but I fixed it."

Edward laughed. "Good for you, Blaxtor."

At Vera's enhanced glare, Edward quieted and gladly progressed partners.

Blaxtor smiled at Vera as he took her hand, but Vera snubbed him. He blinked, taken aback, and then apparently understanding she expected a waltz and thinking Edward, too, was upset about the non-event, Blaxtor gave Edward a wry look and shrugged an apology.

Blushing young lady after blushing young lady passed Edward's way throughout the dance. Some giggled at his touch, some mis-stepped, and some kept their eyes lowered shyly.

He and Vera came back together at the end of the dance and he bowed. "Thank you, my lady."

As he turned to go, the band struck up a waltz and she seized his arm in hers. "Wait. Please, another dance?"

He turned and affecting a look of pain, he tapped his leg. "Alas, I must decline. My injury is playing up after that lively dance."

She pushed in closer to his side. "Of course, how remiss of me. Let us have some refreshments."

Edward nodded and limped with her to the table. He paused as his mother laughed at something Chodstone said upon leaving the room. Edward was about to send her a scowl when she sent her own his way, glowering at his limping leg. Edward grimaced. *Discovered.*

Blaxtor joined them and with a bow to Vera, "Lady Crompton."

"Is your business so very important?"

Edward blanched at her tone. Harvey was a viscount and, as such, her better. He had every right to give her the cut direct she deserved, but instead, he turned to Edward. "I need you in the back parlor." He leaned forward and whispered in Edward's ear. "I think Jameson is too much in his cups. If he keeps going, he will lose his family estates."

"What? Never." Edward faced Vera. "Please excuse me, my lady, but I am needed elsewhere."

"But you haven't finished your champagne."

He put the glass on the table. "I'll join you later."

Both gentlemen gave her a quick bow and strode out of the room. It wasn't until Edward reached the doorway that he realized he had forgotten to keep up his limp. He glanced over his shoulder to see if Vera had noticed, but she was already leading Aubrey out onto the dance floor.

Edward's lips quirked in a smile. Aubrey didn't look at all pleased, while Vera dipped her head at the obviously jealous ladies of the *ton*, some widows, some still married. Had they all set their sights on the Viscount of Grisham? He was surely a catch.

It had been two weeks since Edward met the young American, Miss Elizabeth, and for some reason he was out of sorts. He and his mother never once attended the same event as Chodstone and his ward. He surmised the man was keeping her hidden. After all, every young buck in London would give his eye teeth to have Elizabeth on his arm. Edward realized he was no different and had hoped for another dance with the beautiful American.

During the intervening time, his mother had left London town for Wellsneath and, out from under her watchful eye, Edward tried to 'accidentally' meet Miss Elizabeth. Yet, although he visited all the places society went to see and be seen, he hadn't once set eyes on the beauty.

He tortured himself with thoughts that Chodstone might have already married her and taken her abroad so he could have her all to himself.

With Christmastide over, all of society had now quit London. Whether it was the constant drizzle causing the rising stench in the streets that had him quick to temper, or the empty townhouse where he had no one to talk to except his valet or the other servants, he didn't know.

He decided to go to White's on St James's but on the way stopped his carriage outside Chodstone House, and before he consciously knew what he was doing, he was rapping on Chodstone's door.

The butler answered with a quizzical look. "Can I help you, my lord?"

"I have come to call on His Grace and Miss Davis."

"I am sorry, my lord, but His Grace and Miss Davis have quit London for Chodstone Hall."

"They have left?"

"Yes, my lord."

"Thank you, Hampton."

The disappointment he felt nearly overwhelmed him. But why? He had only met the chit twice. How could she have left such an impression, not only on his mind but on his wayward body? He had to find out. He hadn't been able to concentrate on his work, on politics, on anything. He had to get her out of his system. Perhaps it was time to call on the widow Gordon. Yes, that was where he would go.

Edward stomped to the carriage and said more loudly than needed, "Home, Callow."

⚘

THE NEXT DAY, EDWARD MADE HASTE TO WELLSNEATH IN Summerset. His bay gelding, Rogue, carried him well for six hours but even Edward was tired when they stopped in Carmidge for the night. The next morning a young stable boy, no more than twelve years old, had Rogue saddled and ready in record time. Edward threw the skinny lad a half crown, smiled as the boy's eyes widened at the sight of the coin, and mounted.

It was late evening by the time he arrived at Wellsneath. He handed Rogue over to the groom's care and made his way into the manor.

His butler, Rycroft, met him at the door. "My lord."

Rycroft's tone suggested Edward wasn't expected. Edward supposed he wasn't, but it was his home and he would arrive whenever he found it suitable.

"Is Mother in the parlor?"

"No, my lord. She has retired for the evening."

Edward raised his eyebrow at the butler. It was late but not that late. "Very good, bring a plate and wine to the library."

CHAPTER 8

I zzy sat at the small writing table James had installed in her room and penned her thoughts of country England and society.

She had been at Chodstone Hall two full weeks and, despite Edward's absence, she enjoyed herself immensely. James was a perfect host and had already become a great friend. He'd arranged outings to Bath when the weather permitted and insisted, she buy whatever she wanted. However, other than enjoying the scenery and the goings-on of the people of the time, she couldn't find it in herself to waste his money on what they called fripperies but were just ribbons and such. Especially considering she couldn't take them back with her when she left anyway.

He was always disappointed, but said he understood her reasons.

He had also accepted invitations to soirées where she met many young men, some titled, some not, but all extremely attentive to the new girl in the neighborhood. She liked them all but hoped none would think she was available. She was looking forward to going to The Pump Room. She'd read about it and couldn't wait to experience it personally. Letting out a small laugh, she wondered if the water really did have magical health properties.

Her chest tightened suddenly when Edward's face popped into her head. The dark slashed eyebrows hovering over sultry eyes, and his long eyelashes—so heavy, they seemed to pull his lids down into a sleepy expression. His wide shoulders that she was sure would be well-muscled under her hands if she were ever fortunate enough to touch them.

She sighed and put her pen down. None of the other fine men she had been introduced to had sparked her interest like Edward. Even during the Christmas festivities, the darn man was never far from her mind. And how silly was that? She didn't even know him, and he probably hadn't given her a second thought once she was out of sight. She knew without a doubt, he would have many women at his beck and call.

Even knowing that, even knowing she was being extra silly, she still hoped she would have a chance to go back to London before she returned home. To see him just once more, even if it were just to put a damper on the vision, she had somehow built of him. He can't have been that good-looking, that manly, that hot. It was just her imagination and she had to put the God of Thunder out of her mind once and for all, or she would simply build him up even more when she returned home. Her life would be ruined. How could any modern-day man compete with a dream god?

THAT AFTERNOON, IZZY SAT IN HER RIDICULOUS underclothes as Lucy arranged her hair in a complicated style.

James had accepted an invitation to dinner at Wellsneath Manor. Lady Wellsneath was a lovely person, kind and friendly, and James never passed up a chance to be with her.

Izzy couldn't help but notice the feeling was mutual; the woman's face absolutely lit up the moment she saw James.

Thank goodness James had spent many hours teaching Izzy how to go about in society. For once in her life, she was glad she was naturally shy. It made it easier to be quiet when she heard something she didn't like, though she often had to bite her tongue. The men and women of that time really needed to get more exciting lives.

Despite the fact she thought she had managed great restraint, James warned her more than once, she should exert better control of her facial expressions and body language, as well as her speech.

She pulled at the corset.

"Please try to be still, miss."

"Lucy." Izzy drew out her name as a reprimand. She had told the girl a million times to call her by her name and not 'miss'.

"Try to be still, Izzy."

The petticoat wasn't so bad, and the corset was acceptable as part of the dress of this time—even if being able to breathe entailed a fight with Lucy not to pull it so tight. And the stays holding her stockings up even felt a little sexy. But Izzy drew a line at the choice of bloomers or nothing.

Izzy smoothed her dress over her lap.

Apparently, most Regency women didn't wear underwear and the ones who did, wore gross bloomers. Lucy had assured Izzy that more and more ladies of society wore bloomers, but that didn't stop her wondering whether every woman she met wore any underwear. She hoped none of the bloomer-less women took a fall.

The moment they arrived at Chodstone Hall; James had arranged for Izzy to meet the best dressmaker in Bath—a mantua-maker he called her. She measured Izzy to within an inch of her life and made a stunning wardrobe for her. But

Izzy still insisted on no bloomers, so James had agreed to allow his in-house seamstress to entertain Izzy's strange requests. Thankfully, he had ordered the lady's maid and the seamstress not to make this known to anyone, not even the seamstress's own husband.

The seamstress acknowledged that she and her husband, a footman, would lose their positions if she ever spoke about making more of the strange underclothes Izzy showed her. She had shown the seamstress the underwear she had worn when she arrived, and although she made them quite a bit larger than the original, Izzy was happy with the seamstress's efforts.

Lucy pushed a pin into Izzy's head. "Ouch... do you mean to use my skull to attach the pins?"

"Sorry, Miss Eliz..." Izzy frowned and Lucy repented. "Izzy."

Izzy rubbed her head but smiled. "It's okay. You're really not as bad as some hairdressers I've had."

"Thank you." Lucy grinned at Izzy's reflection in the mirror. "You do talk funny sometimes."

"Yeah, I suppose. Although, English people talk funny to me."

Izzy chose the lavender evening gown and was thankful for Lucy's help. There was no way she could button the thing up at the back by herself.

The material was so thin it was practically see-through, and Izzy was scared she'd put her nails straight through it. No wonder they had to wear petticoats.

All ready, Izzy gazed at her reflection in the mirror. The dress was lovely, although the neckline was a little lower than Izzy would have liked. She didn't like calling attention to her small attributes. From her experience in her own time period, men preferred their women more robust.

She liked Lady Alice Wellsneath, although whether that

was because she was Edward's mother or just a nice woman, Izzy wasn't sure. She supposed Lady Wellsneath was a highly respected member of the *ton* but wondered about James's feelings about his neighbor. Alice was at every festivity they attended. Of course, Izzy guessed that was to be expected anyway. Still, James seemed to also visit Wellsneath Manor quite a bit.

Her nerves started vibrating at the thought of the other guests. If any of the other social engagements had told her anything, the gentry could be awful snobs. She hoped Lady Wellsneath had invited someone charming to be her partner for the night.

Izzy descended the wide curved staircase, a princess in a children's fairytale. The large foyer beckoned her into its stately embrace. Chodstone Hall was much warmer than Chodstone House in London. The portraits of Chodstone's ancestors she passed on the way down were joyful faces, caught in moments of time, doing happy things. A well-dressed man pushing a boy on a swing, a woman sitting on a blanket, nursing a baby and smiling at another small boy. Izzy loved gazing at the pictures.

So much love exuded from them, she wished she had more photographs of her parents and siblings captured in happy moments.

The foyer itself was both regal, with its gigantic chandelier and ultra-white tiled floor, and warmly elegant, with hangings of landscapes and hunting parties on the walls.

James walked out of the library as Izzy neared the bottom of the staircase. He stopped and waited for her, his gaze admiring.

"You look beautiful, my dear."

Stepping onto the floor, she placed her hand on the arm he held out for her and tipped her head slightly in acknowledgement just as he had taught her. "Why thank you, Your Grace."

"Very good, but please call me Chodstone. You are my ward after all, and people expect you to address me so."

She nodded. "Very well."

Sanderson, Chodstone Hall's very proper butler, held the door open for them and they strolled outside. For once the night sky was clear and Izzy welcomed the stars silently.

James helped her into the curricle and they were on their way.

"How far is Wellsneath Manor?"

"About four miles." He checked the time on his pocket watch. "Alice is expecting us at eight and we should arrive just before then."

Izzy was nervous. Had Edward changed his mind? Would he be there?

However, when James had afternoon tea with Alice the day before, he'd been assured that Edward still stayed on in London. Izzy didn't know whether to be disappointed by that fact or glad. She liked looking at him, but Edward unsettled her with the way he gazed at her as if he were curious—and curiosity where she was concerned was not welcomed, not by her, nor by James.

Less than half an hour passed, and they were driving along a gravel path lined by perfectly trimmed hedges. It was too dark to see the countryside, but Izzy knew for certain it would be breathtaking in its blanket of white snow.

The carriage stopped in front of the manor. Three stories high and with a wide, double-doored entrance above two wider steps. It was smaller than Chodstone Hall but just as beautiful. The gas lights lit up the pale stone façade with a welcoming gaiety.

The footman placed a stair and opened the door. James stepped out and little snowflakes landed in his hair. He held his hand for Izzy to step down. "Inside quickly before consumption finds you."

The hair on the back of Izzy's neck tingled and she scanned the area for the reason. A curtain fell in place over a front window. Someone had just let it go. They were being watched.

Hoping Alice was as nice in her own home as she had been at the other festivities where her manners were scrutinized every second, Izzy let James lead her to the door that opened the moment their feet touched the first step.

The butler bowed. "Your Grace, Miss Elizabeth, Lady Wellsneath is waiting for you in the front parlor."

"Thank you, Rycroft. I know the way."

Once Izzy had removed her coat, James guided her through a beautifully furnished hall. A single staircase curved up to the second floor and the hall continued under it to the back of the house. Small tables and chairs stood against the dark wood panels, above which the walls were painted in a pretty lemon. Landscape wall hangings broke the yellow. She was especially taken with one depicting a pond that was expansive enough to hold a few canoes carrying prettily dressed women holding parasols above their heads and perfectly attired gentlemen rowing them from one side to an island in the middle. She hoped that one day she would get to see that scene with her own eyes.

James led her into a charmingly decorated pale blue sitting room. Plush chairs and settees cozied around a fireplace. On the mantel sat two vases full of blue and white flowers. Izzy decided it was definitely a woman's room.

The woman in question stood up at their entrance. "James," Alice said, moving forward to greet them. "How good to see you." She took his hands and kissed him on each cheek then stepped back. "And Miss Davis. I have been looking forward to getting to know more about you."

CALLIE BERKHAM BERKHAM

Izzy curtsied as best she could, but the tiny hairs on the back of her neck stiffened once more. Her gaze darted behind Alice and she brought the curtsy up short. Edward stood resting his elbow on the fireplace mantel. Their eyes locked for a long instant until his gaze swept down her body from head to toe and back again. He arched his brow and dipped his head slightly forward.

His penetrating gaze had her every nerve end tingling. His lazy brown eyes warmed, telling her he liked what he saw, and the heat in her cheeks told her she was blushing. Why did she have to blush so frequently, especially now? Izzy didn't know whether to be happy he was there or not, but her heart sang a joyous tune.

Alice continued talking. "You are as beautiful as ever, Miss Elizabeth."

Izzy felt comfortable in Alice's company, and putting Edward from her mind, smiled at her hostess. "Thank you. Please call me Izzy."

"That would not be proper."

Izzy laughed. "Of course."

Edward strode forward, shook James's hand. "Chodstone."

"Wellsneath."

Taking Izzy's gloved hand, Edward bowed as he kissed the back of it. Even through the glove she felt his warm breath as he spoke, and more tingles flitted up her arm.

"Pleased to meet you again, Miss Elizabeth."

Izzy had to snap herself out of her frozen state and quickly curtsied. "My lord."

His eyes darkened in what she could only guess was anger. Maybe he adhered to social formality more than she had thought he would. He seemed irritated that she nearly forgot to curtsy to him as his eyes swept over her head. She fought the urge to step back. Why was he always so cross with her?

She sucked in her bottom lip. What right did he have to mess with her like that?

Just then the butler announced another guest, who swept into the room before being properly announced. "The Lady Vera Crompton."

Alice excused herself to go to her newest guest.

Izzy was stunned by Lady Crompton's beauty. Her dark hair was fashioned in a high style with ringlets bordering a perfectly formed oval face. Her eyes were large and brown, and they focused on Edward, calling him to her side. Her emerald green gown was again cut low, much lower than Izzy's, and the lady had much more flesh to contain than Izzy. Instead of falling loosely from under her bust, the thin material fitted perfectly to her figure until the fabric met her hips, where it then fell to just above her green slippers.

Izzy dragged her gaze away. The dress left nothing to the imagination and from Edward's darkening eyes, he thought so too.

A tendril of what could only be jealousy wound through Izzy's chest. She silently slapped herself. She had never had cause to mentally hit herself over a man before. Oh, she often did the silent slap when speaking at meetings where her nervousness had her blurting out any number of stupid things—jokes to her, but they only caused others to look at her as if she were mad. But here, in this time, she would be black and blue if she were really slapping herself.

She looked at the toes of her pretty green slippers. She had no right to feel any emotion for the Earl of Wellsneath, let alone jealousy. She didn't know the man and even if she did, even if he was attracted to her, she couldn't get involved with him. She would soon be gone, and he needed to marry a suitable lady, someone like the gorgeous Lady Crompton.

Edward appeared to school his expression into one of formality while eyeing the woman. Obviously, it wasn't polite to leer at a guest—no matter how hot she was—in mixed company. He strode to stand beside his mother to welcome the Lady Vera Crompton.

However, noticing the way Vera linked her arm in Edward's and pushed up so close, her breast flattened against his upper arm, Izzy wondered if she was indeed a lady. Again, she admonished herself. She didn't know the woman. Why had her cat claws unsheathed? She may well be a lovely person, a perfect match for Edward. She was a lady, after all, and Izzy was just a commoner to them, a nobody. He was way out of her league anyway, and even if she were of that time, she would never have made a suitable match for him.

Moving to the window, she gazed out into the night. Why she thought she would fit into their company, she didn't know. She doubted there was any time or place she would ever completely fit in.

While she was daydreaming, James took her arm in his. "Huh?" she said.

"You are wool gathering." Concern filled his eyes, although he smiled encouragingly. "Time to go in for dinner."

"Of course." Izzy's eyes darted to the backs of Edward and Vera as they walked through an open door leading to the dining room.

She forced a smile onto her face as James took Alice's arm into his free one.

"It seems we are not to have the correct numbers and I, for one, am glad. This way I have two of the most beautiful women in Britain to escort into dinner."

Alice let out a small, genteel laugh. "Thank you." She regarded Izzy with a twinkle in her eyes. "His Grace likes to see reactions at his compliments."

Izzy caught on to her teasing. "You are a rake, sir."

"Me? Never. Perhaps when I was young." He glanced at Alice with a conspiratorial look. "But not any longer."

A slight blush of pink highlighted Alice's cheekbones as they entered the dining room. The room was narrower than the one in Chodstone Hall, but still had ample room for a sideboard nearly as long as the table that would seat twelve people comfortably, and enough space for the staff to walk behind the pulled-out chairs.

More dark wood paneling filled the lower half of the walls but in that room the upper half was painted a pretty shade of carnation pink. A large portrait of a beautiful but sad-eyed woman hung over the sideboard. Izzy glanced at Alice then back to the painting. The subject was most definitely a younger Alice. Izzy wondered what had made her so melancholic that the artist couldn't ignore it.

Just then Alice laughed at something James said. The difference in her appearance had nothing to do with age. This woman was happy.

Edward sat at the head of the table with Vera on his left with her back to the sideboard. James waited for the footman to seat Alice on Edward's right. Another footman guided Izzy to the seat beside Vera, while James sat beside Alice.

While their numbers were uneven, the seating arrangements worked because if there had been a sixth, he would not have had a person opposite his seat.

James drew Alice into conversation about the latest *ton* gossip while Vera all but turned her back on Izzy to talk to Edward about the current fashions. While he answered her numerous questions, his gaze flitted more than once to Izzy, who tried her best not to look at him.

Course after course was set out in front of her, and while Izzy enjoyed the spring lamb, she didn't much like the pheasant—neither the taste nor the smell. James noticed her pushing the meat around her plate.

"It is somewhat of an acquired taste," James said with a knowing smile.

Izzy pushed her plate away. "I think you are right."

Vera looked down her straight nose at Izzy. "You have not dined on pheasant before?"

Izzy colored, feeling even more out of place. She gave what she hoped wasn't a nervous laugh. "No, and I hope never to again."

James and Alice laughed, and Izzy was sure the corners of Edward's mouth twitched with humor, but Vera huffed.

Izzy decided then and there, she didn't like Lady Crompton. The woman was a snobby cow. Izzy hid her thoughts behind a polite smile and thankfully accepted a piece of apple pie from the footman, who spooned clotted cream over the hot slice. The aroma wafted up into Izzy's nostrils and her mouth began watering before she enjoyed the first spoonful.

Between furtive glances in Edward's direction, Izzy savored every bite of the dessert. Only the sound of her name coming from Vera's mouth had her hand stilling before it reached her plate to scoop up another spoonful.

She glanced up at the horror-filled faces of Edward and Alice. "Did I do something?"

"Not at all," James said. "Vera was just telling us the latest *on-dit* of the *ton*."

Izzy put down her spoon. "And it's about me?"

"Us, actually. It seems certain members of the *ton* think we are engaged to be married."

Izzy glanced at Edward whose eyes hid behind puckered brows. Though she could hardly see them, she felt the daggers they were shooting at her.

"What? How the..." Izzy snapped her mouth shut before the curse escaped. "How did they come up with that rubbish?"

Vera sat back, and Izzy's hand itched to swipe the smug look from her face. She'd apparently chosen the wrong words to show her anger. Darn. She had to think harder before she spoke.

James gave her a wink.

Izzy quickly glanced at Edward. He'd seen James wink and by the tic in his rigidly set jaw, he thought the rumor true.

"Do not let it bother you," James said. "They will know the truth soon enough."

Izzy frowned. What did James mean by that?

After dinner, they retired to the back parlor. Izzy was surprised the men remained with the women. She thought they went to the library or somewhere to smoke and drink. While she understood the smoking, she considered drinking in mixed company to be entertainment. Huh, entertainment. She couldn't help a smile forming on her lips as she sat next to Alice on the settee in front of the cozy fire. She was even starting to think like them.

The butler placed a tray with a bottle of champagne and five glasses on the low table.

Alice nodded, and the bottle popped with a soulful hiss. Alice stood up and accepted the first glass. "Thank you, Rycroft."

Once everyone had their glass, Izzy was about to sip hers but stopped as Alice spoke.

"I thought it would be nice to toast Miss Elizabeth Davis, ward of the Duke of Chodstone." She raised her glass. "Welcome to England, Miss Davis."

Circles of heat warmed Izzy's cheeks. Edward raised his brows as he stood beside the fireplace with one elbow resting on the corner of the mantel and held up his glass. "To Miss Elizabeth Davis."

James stepped to Alice's side. "Thank you, Alice." He held his glass up to Izzy. "To Elizabeth."

Izzy dared not look at Edward but gazed at Vera instead. The woman had installed herself in a chair that sat so close to

Edward that all he had to do was look down to see her ample cleavage.

The woman's eyes narrowed in spite and with a fake smile plastered on her lips, she held out her glass without a word.

Vera was obviously used to being the center of attention.

"Thank you," Izzy said. "I'm enjoying England immensely and hope to see more of the countryside before I leave."

"You're leaving?" Vera said. "But I thought you would live here now that you are the ward of a duke."

She had no idea what to say to that. The reason she was there was because her parents had died. That much was true. And having become James's ward, she now lived in his home and country.

Izzy widened her eyes at James.

He chuckled. "Elizabeth has to go back to oversee arrangements to her parents' estates but will return to England after she has accomplished all that she needs to in America."

Izzy nodded and thanked James with her eyes.

Vera watched the exchange between Izzy and James and asked in her high and mighty tone, "And will you be accompanying Miss Davis on the voyage, Your Grace?"

James's expression never changed, except Izzy noted the slight wrinkles of ire around his eyes before he replied. "Perhaps."

Vera gave Edward a 'told-you-so' look.

Clearing his throat, James held his hand out to Izzy. "Would you accompany me for a stroll in the gardens? It's not so cold now that the snow has stopped falling, and Wellsneath has a most famous statue I'm sure you would love."

Keeping as controlled as possible, Izzy stood up and placed her hand on his offered arm. "Thank you. I couldn't think of anything nicer."

They walked through the open French doors and once

they'd spanned the wide patio, they descended the three steps onto one of the garden's many paths. Someone had been hard at work clearing the snow, so it was nearly completely dry. Although it was altogether too cold for Izzy, she didn't complain.

Soft, yellow lights lit their way as they strolled along in silence. Izzy couldn't see much beyond the lights, but the layer of snow nestling over and under the perfectly trimmed hedges told her there probably wouldn't be any color in the garden at that time of year.

Once she was sure the others could no longer hear, Izzy said, "Vera isn't going to let the rumor that you and I are engaged alone. If you ask me, she's bent on proving it's true."

The chuckle James emitted shook his whole body, including his arm and Izzy's hand. "Do not trouble yourself with gossip."

She was about to argue that it could hurt his reputation, but they came to a stop in front of a gigantic statue of a stately noble. "Who is that?" she asked.

He grinned down at her. "That is Edward's great-grandfather, Lord Wellsneath. He was one of the parliamentarians who brought about the Coronation Act that was passed in 1689, calling for all future monarchs to make a solemn oath to preserve the laws and statutes of the land. If you are interested, there are books in the library that explain what happened, but suffice to say, after the lords, including Wellsneath, spoke to William, fear of civil war ceased, King William and Queen Mary became joint monarchs, and a new parliament began."

"And the point of this history lesson?"

"The point, my dear, is that if you had arrived in the seventeenth century, you would have had a far different experience than now. See? While Lord Wellsneath, his cohorts, and the then king and queen are all dead in this time period, they would have been very much alive then. I hear he was a handsome man, more so than even Edward, and it is quite feasible that you could have developed a tendre for that Lord Wellsneath."

Izzy wanted to argue, but his point was made.

Her chest tightened as emotions formed a knot in her throat. The subject of the statue was dead and along with him, his wife. Tears filled her eyes as she looked up at her guardian.

The concerned encouragement in his eyes told her he was glad his lesson hadn't gone unheard. He and everyone there would be dead when she returned home, and she would be able to read about their lives in history books.

She glanced back into the house. Alice was flipping through a magazine while Edward and Vera seemed to be in deep conversation. He was meant to marry someone in that era—had already married, probably had children, and been buried well before Izzy was born. She let out a long heartfelt sigh. "I understand."

"Good. I knew you were as intelligent as your parents. Now, I would like to tell you a secret."

A grin broke out on Izzy's face. She loved secrets. "A secret?"

"You must promise not to disclose it to anyone, especially Edward, at this time."

She quickly crossed her heart. "I won't."

He turned her so she faced him. "I have asked Alice to marry me and she has agreed."

"Really? That's great." She threw her arms around his neck and gave him a hug. "She's wonderful." Releasing him, she stepped back and eyed him. "I hope I'll be here for the celebrations."

"We hope so too."

She gave him a peck on the cheek. "Why is it a secret though?"

"Alice wants to see Edward settled first. In case you haven't noticed, he has a low opinion of me."

"I have noticed his coldness actually. Why?"

"It's a long story that goes back many years, but the main point is his father always detested me because he knew where Alice's affections lay. He hounded Alice's poor father into agreeing to their match and, in turn, her bed-bound father used emotional blackmail to make her acquiesce." He gazed into the distance. "Had I been a duke then, mayhap things would have been different, but none of us can see into the future." He smiled at Izzy. "Except you of course."

Izzy giggled. "Well, I'm no seer, but shush. What if someone heard you?"

He shrugged. "No one could understand such a thing; even I still have trouble coming to terms with what your parents are capable of."

"Edward's father sounds like an awful man."

"He was a beast to Alice, but he loved his sons."

Izzy hugged James again. "She's lucky to have you then."

CHAPTER 9

E dward hardly heard a word Vera said. He was trying to watch Chodstone and Elizabeth, wishing he had thought to add more lights to the garden.

"What is the matter?" Vera said with a pout. "You are brooding."

"Hmm? Ah, yes, I had some bad news today."

"Tell me about it."

"No." He straightened. "I think I need some fresh air. Mother will keep you company."

At that, he strode through the doors and, trying not to look like he was following Chodstone, passed the path his guests took and meandered along the patio and down the steps to another path. They all intersected at the statue anyway.

He stopped short, pretending to admire the great oak his grandfather had planted the day he married Edward's grandmother. What was the duke doing out there? Chodstone never had refuted the allegations that he was to marry. He had actually appeared pleased at the prospect.

Edward kicked the bottom of the trunk. Why should he

care if Chodstone courted his ward? The man was free to marry any of his choosing, and Elizabeth would have a comfortable life as his wife. A man's age had nothing to do with arranging suitable matches. His own father had taken a young debutante as his bride.

He glanced back toward the parlor, but from that angle, he could see nothing of his mother. She had been an unhappy bride, he knew that, but even she admitted the late Earl of Wellsneath had been a wonderful father to him and Thomas. He'd always made time to teach them riding, hunting, shooting, or sword fighting. Even when busy with his mistresses, if either son had needed him, he'd been there for them.

EVEN SO, HIS CHEST TIGHTENED AT THE THOUGHT OF Chodstone bedding the young Elizabeth. He had never had such a confusing jumble of emotions roiling within him. Why should he care? He didn't even know her. Edward rubbed the back of his neck. There was more to Miss Elizabeth Davis than what was apparent, he was certain of it.

Before he was aware of what he was doing, he found himself strolling toward the statue. The path ahead curved to the left and the shrubs offered him a refuge from their eyes. However, before he could reach them, Vera came alongside.

"There you are. I began to worry when I lost sight of you. You just don't seem yourself tonight, and I would like to offer what comfort I can."

The last thing he wanted was company at that moment, especially Vera's. She was much too cloying. He wanted to be rude to her but that wasn't the honorable thing to do, so he smiled. "Thank you. I would like very much not to talk but to stay in my thoughts for a time longer."

She wrapped her arm in his. "Of course, darling. We'll just amble silently for a while."

Stopping at the shrub of refuge, he pretended to be interested in the new winter-loving groundcover the gardener had procured from the south of France. It was quite unremarkable in the night, but the tiny lavender flowers would open come morning and afford a magnificent display. He wondered what Elizabeth would think of them.

Vera gasped and he looked up. She had her hand over her mouth to stop the sound from escaping any further, and her eyes were wide with laughter as she stared through the outer branches of the shrub.

Edward followed her gaze, but the statue wasn't what had caught her attention. To the left and, although in the shadows, he could quite plainly make out Elizabeth in Chodstone's arms.

His chest tightened so much he couldn't breathe at the sight of her accepting his affections.

"It is true," Vera whispered. "The American isn't just his ward after all. But surely, he wouldn't marry her. She isn't titled, probably no more than a bluestocking. He must be hoping to make her his mistress."

Without thinking, Edward stepped around the shrub and, striding forward, said, "Sorry to interrupt such an intimate moment, but Mother was wondering if you would like a drink before you leave."

Vera hurried after him.

Chodstone and Elizabeth parted, but to Edward's mind it was Chodstone that initiated the move, not Elizabeth. Did she not know how compromising their actions were? She appeared confused but not flustered, as any other young debutante would be. No blush touched her cheeks. She wasn't even embarrassed at being caught in such an act.

She had no shame as she smiled brightly at Edward. "We'd love a drink, wouldn't we, James?"

James looked at Edward and Vera with his piercing brown eyes.

Edward assumed the duke wasn't pleased at being interrupted in his roguish ways and

stabbed him with a hard look of his own. He had the most pressing urge to call him out. But why? What did he care? Even if he did, it was too late now. The man had to marry the girl or risk her reputation before she even had her coming out.

Chodstone straightened to his full height and, smoothing his hands down the front of his jacket, gave a small bow of his head only. "Wellsneath, Lady Crompton."

Chodstone took Elizabeth's hand and kissed the back of it as he bowed. "I will see you inside."

"All right."

The girl's surprised eyes watched him stride back to the house. "He must have just remembered something important," she said, almost to herself, then turned that bright smile back to Edward and Vera. "It's a beautiful night, isn't it? I was starting to think it never stopped raining or snowing in England."

The butler made himself known by clearing his throat. "Lady Wellsneath asks if Lady Crompton could join her in the front parlor."

Vera glanced from Edward to Elizabeth. "Now?"

"Yes, my lady."

She let out an irritated huff and began to leave but stopped and turned around. "Are you coming, Edward?"

"You go ahead."

Her mouth opened to speak but closed again. She twirled around and flounced past Rycroft toward the house.

Edward watched her without seeing her, his mind filled with thoughts of Elizabeth. He wanted to demand she tell him about her relationship with Chodstone. His jaw tightened, and he felt the familiar tic pulse there. He couldn't be so rude, but more to the point, he had no right to demand anything of her. He knew he should take her back into the house, but something stirred in his stomach at the thought of sharing her again with Chodstone.

"Would you like to see the maze?"

Her face opened in a true smile as her blue eyes widened. He neither sensed nor saw any deception there.

"I'd love to." However, a tiny frown drew her perfectly groomed eyebrows closer together. "Do all country houses have mazes?"

He couldn't stop the chuckle rumbling in his chest. "Not all, but most."

"Don't get me wrong, I love them, but I have to wonder why."

He tipped his head to indicate they should walk, and as they strolled around the statue they walked through the high hedges into the maze.

Edward had to concentrate to keep his voice even. Her closeness was doing something to his insides and her floral scent, an aroma he could not name, buzzed through his senses.

"It is an entertainment. However, its real purpose is to allow people to take exercise without realizing they are doing so."

"Ah, I suppose people prefer to stay indoors because of the cold. It's hardly ever cold where I come from."

The way she said the last told Edward she was thinking fondly of her faraway home.

"You miss your home? I am inclined to think you mean not to return to England when you go back to America."

"James wants me to stay of course, but I have family there and I know I'll miss them if I stay away too long."

It was Edward's turn to frown. Family? He had assumed

Elizabeth had no family. Why else would she be made Chodstone's ward?

"But why are you not with your family then? Why have you come here and why are you Chodstone's ward?"

He felt her stiffen beside him.

"Oh, yes... um... my parents died, and it was their wish I come and live with my guardian. But I do have a brother and two sisters who are prepared to take me in."

"I'm sorry about your parents."

She shrugged as if it did not signify. "That's okay. Tell me about you. What's it like being an earl?"

He laughed again. She had a way of asking the most impolite questions in the most delightful way. It was as if she did not know which questions were acceptable and which were not.

"I'm sorry. Was that rude?"

"As we are alone, you are forgiven."

"James has tried to teach me how to behave when in the company of gentry and royals, but you have so many rules here. I'm glad I don't have to live by them my whole life."

"Are you not here to make a suitable match? Mayhap with a titled gentleman?"

"What? No. I'm here to enjoy some time with James, not to get married." She cocked her head to look up at him with those wide blue eyes. "Are you on the lookout for a wife?"

His brows rose unbidden at her speech.

"No. I am not on the *lookout* for a wife." He frowned. No American he had met spoke like she did. "I have visited America and I cannot recall ever hearing someone speak like you."

She picked a daphne bud. Edward could tell from her ever-moving startled eyes she was trying to think of an excuse.

"I come from a small isolated community and I suppose

our speech has developed quite differently to those in the large cities."

"Interesting."

She was intriguing, and Edward was stunned how well he could read her. She wasn't exactly lying, but her words were chosen as a generalization and not a reason for her speech.

"What about you? What does an earl do with his time? What sort of things do you enjoy?"

Ah, a change of subject. Edward smiled and allowed it, but he couldn't shake the idea that there was something quite strange about her, something he couldn't quite put his finger on.

"I have my seat here in the country. The tenants and upkeep of the estate I attend to. I also have my duty to the Parliament in London as a member of the House of Lords."

"Do you like politics?"

He gazed down into her plainly interested eyes. She wanted to know about him, what he liked. No woman had ever been slightly interested in his life other than his title and fortune. She had said so herself. She wasn't interested in gaining a titled match. He wondered what it would be like to be married to someone who cared for him and not his title.

"Why yes, I find that I indeed do."

"Good."

She stopped and turned her face up to him. He peered into her eyes, trying to look behind their warm blue beauty, trying to see the woman behind the not terribly well-constructed masquerade.

Her eyes darkened, sky blue to royal blue.

"It... it would be just awful to have to do something you don't enjoy."

Her Cupid's bow mouth remained slightly open. Edward didn't know if she swayed toward him or he toward her, but before he knew what he was doing, his lips were on her soft, warm mouth. She parted her lips, inviting him in. He accepted the invitation and, spreading his hands on her upper and lower back, pulled her in to his body where she fit perfectly.

The moan deep in his throat stirred his senses. He fought his traitorous body and pushed her away. She teetered, confused eyes piercing him, stabbing him with guilt. How could he mistreat her so? Where was his honor, the honor he carried proudly that stood him apart from his father? He would not ruin an innocent to satisfy his own carnal desires.

CHAPTER 10

I zzy blinked, trying to regain the use of the treacherous muscles in her legs that seemed to have turned to mush around her shaky bones. She had to stay upright. Staring at Edward, who rubbed his palms down his face, she couldn't believe she had all but thrown herself at him. She'd never done anything like that before in her life. Usually the men who wanted to kiss her had to do all the work. She shut her eyes at the memory of standing on tiptoe and searching out his mouth as if she had to taste him or regret forever a lost opportunity.

The moment their lips met, she sank into oblivion, feeling only his warm heat and tasting his warm breath tinged with whisky and the apple pie. Her body had melted against his firm frame, feeling his hard muscles bunching as she tried to get closer to him.

She blinked again. Why had he pushed her away? She had never enjoyed such an amazingly awesome kiss in her life, and she hadn't wanted it to end. The cold air resting on her arms made them ache with emptiness.

He gave her a chagrined look. "I apologize. That was most improper of me and it won't happen again."

Not happen again? Why? Didn't he like it? She tried to wrap her head around what he had said. It was improper. Of course, if touching was improper in this time, kissing surely had to be. *Vera didn't seem to think it improper to touch though. Had he kissed her?* They did seem close and Izzy wondered just how close.

None of your business, Izzy. He and Vera were most likely courting. That's what they did in those days. Court and then marry. Izzy was ashamed of herself for leading Edward on like that. She wasn't going to be around forever, and he had to make a suitable match with a highborn lady and she definitely wasn't highborn. In fact, if she had been born in this time period, she would probably be in some kind of service. So darn far below Edward, he shouldn't even be anywhere near her, let alone dining and strolling in an empty garden maze and kissing.

"Edward," Vera's voice sounded around the corner of the hedge wall.

Izzy turned her back to Edward and gasped. She hadn't even noticed they had made it to the centre of the maze, and she stood ogling the ugliest statue she had ever seen. A small but grotesque-looking pig sat on a waist-high plinth. Izzy half expected it to lunge for her throat, it was so hideously hostile.

"Ah, there you are, Edward."

Izzy spun on her heels in time to see Vera take Edward's arm in hers, clearly demonstrating he was her property. Her eyes narrowed at Izzy and, as if connected, her top lip raised in a sneering and threatening aspect that rivaled the pig's hideous expression.

"James is looking for you."

Izzy gazed at Edward; he was studying her with amused eyes, so he couldn't have seen Vera's hostility.

"You have found the prize at the centre of the maze," he said to Izzy.

"Prize? It's the most grotesque thing I've ever seen." Izzy couldn't help but glance at Vera as she said it but immediately felt guilty for doing so. Vera wasn't ugly, but the woman certainly had a vile personality.

"It is," Edward said, holding in his mirth. "George has helped welcome the Wellsneaths' visitors to the maze for centuries."

"George?"

"That is the pig's name," Vera said, her smug expression letting Izzy know she had personal knowledge of Wellsneath Manor. "As I said, James is looking for you."

※

Izzy stared at her reflection in the mirror as Lucy expertly coiffured her long blonde hair in a loose bun at the nape of her neck, letting Izzy's natural curls hang loose to frame her face so they softened what could have been a severe hairstyle.

Three days. Three days since James had welcomed his houseguests to Chodstone Hall and all Izzy could think about was Edward and that kiss. He had apologized, saying it was improper. But even though she knew they wouldn't be together long, she still didn't want his apologies, she didn't want him worrying about propriety where she was concerned. He was worried about ruining her, but he didn't know she was from a time where there was no such thing as being ruined by a simple kiss. A shiver ran down her back. Not that their kiss was simple; it was the most exciting kiss Izzy had ever had.

Although she knew it was wrong—not so much for her, but for Edward—she had done her best to be alone with him again, hoping he would do the dishonorable thing and kiss her again. She screwed up her nose at her reflection. Every time they found themselves in one another's company, someone interrupted them. And the most troublesome someone was Vera.

"There you are, miss. Do you like it?"

Izzy snapped her eyes to Lucy. "It's perfect. Thank you."

As Lucy helped her into a pretty pastel blue day dress, Izzy silently berated herself. It was all right for her to have a flirtation, but for Edward, it could only mean gossip if they were found in a compromising position again. He was all but engaged to the Lady Vera Crompton and Izzy had no right to come between them. How many times did she have to tell herself, she was there to observe, not interfere? Eighteen-eleven was already past history in her world, and she had to keep reminding herself that when she returned to the future, they would all be dead.

However, Izzy couldn't help but wonder what kind of life Edward would have with Vera. The woman was a cold thing. So cold, a chill at the thought of her crept along Izzy's arms.

"You are cold, miss." Lucy handed her a short jacket—ah... a *Spencer*.

Izzy shook her head and pushed the jacket away. "No. I'm not really cold."

The maid gave her an I-don't-believe-you look but took the jacket away.

James was hosting a ball that night and everyone who was anyone would be there. Izzy smiled inwardly. Maybe, *no Izzy, mayhap*: she really had to think in their archaic way of speaking so it would sound natural when she spoke. Mayhap she could find someone warmer for Edward, someone who wasn't out for his title and money, someone who would care for him as much as Izzy did.

She started.

She cared for him? Of course, she did. He was a nice man,

a friend. No matter what time period she met him, she would have liked him; she was sure of it.

As she thought about finding a nice girl for him, something niggled the back of her mind. Something she had never felt before, even when her fiancé had told her he was in love with her best friend. Even so, she knew its name... jealousy. No, it couldn't be.

Great.

"Anything else, miss?"

"No, thanks, that will be all."

She sighed as Lucy closed the door behind her. *Step back, Izzy.* That was the right thing to do. No interfering. No trying to match him with someone else. After all, Edward's mother liked Vera, so there had to be something admirable about her. Either that, or Alice wasn't a good judge of character.

Izzy was still thinking of Edward as she made her way down the stairs from the third floor.

Before she descended the second set of stairs to the ground floor, James waylaid her.

"Could I have a word with you, Elizabeth?"

"Sure... um... yes."

Izzy followed James into the library on the second floor. A fire warmed the dark wood paneling and dark furniture. His expression was dour as he indicated the sofa, and Izzy sat down, back straight, her hands clasped in her lap.

Had she done something wrong? She couldn't think of anything. She was always careful of her speech and deportment and she was certain she had improved greatly in that regard.

He sat beside her and frowned into the fireplace as if it had been built wrongly.

Izzy couldn't take the silence any longer. "What's the matter?"

He cleared his throat as if he was going to launch into a speech. Or lecture, Izzy thought with irritation.

"I had hoped not to talk about this again, but I have noticed your continued inclination toward Edward."

Izzy widened her eyes at that. "My inclination? Well yeah, I like him, if that's what you mean."

"That is what I mean. I think perhaps you should not spend so much time in his company. You do realize Alice has high hopes for a match with Vera?"

"And I'm sure Vera has high hopes too." Izzy gave James a mischievous glance. "That is, if she can't find a better match."

"Your meaning?"

"Oh, James, you must have noticed how she flirts with you. If you even looked like coming around, she would dump Edward in a heartbeat. Even I know, a duke is a better catch than an earl."

James laughed. "I do love the way you talk, and your intelligence benefits you greatly but, in this instance, I think you are exaggerating her friendliness. After all, when I marry Alice and she marries Edward, we will be family."

Izzy stared into the fire. He was right. Their lives were already formatted. She had no right, but something clicked in Izzy's mind then. Why couldn't she find love in the nineteenth century? Abby had in the eighteenth.

"There is no possibility you and Edward can make a match, Elizabeth. You are not of this time and I fear what would happen if you interfered in the space-time continuum."

"Mom and Dad told you about that, huh?"

He dipped his head in answer.

"Well, forget that for a moment and remember I told you about Abby? How she stayed in 1746 Scotland and nothing happened."

"We cannot be certain of that. Had she not stayed, would this world be different?"

Izzy smiled. "I guess we'll never know."

"That is my point. Abby doesn't signify at this time; you do. You must return to your own time once this house party is over."

"But that's only another week." Izzy's voice rose in panic. "I still haven't met Jane Austen and I'm not going to have the chance unless I go back to London. I thought we were going to go back so I could experience what the season is like."

"I am afraid that is no longer possible. You are becoming too fond of this era... and Edward."

She couldn't argue with that. He was right on all counts. But there was no way she was leaving before meeting Jane Austen. What was the point in being there if she didn't? Nothing, that was what. Plus, she was only halfway through her book and she needed to do more research. She had been making copious amounts of notes in case Garrett and Max found a way to pull her back before she could finish, but she never thought James would insist she return to her time.

"I still haven't finished my book. What if I promise I'll try to get along with Vera the Cold?" At James's dark look, Izzy recanted. "I'm sorry. That was uncalled for."

"I will make a decision at the end of the week." He tapped the tip of her nose with the pad of his index finger. "I will be watching you."

She screwed up her nose and leaned back. *Well, that was a little too condescending.* "I'm not a child, James, and while I'm grateful you agreed to have me as your guest while I'm here, I would like to be treated like a grown woman. You have to remember, where I come from, I make my own way and I make a good living. You might call me a bluestocking, but everyone works in the future, and women make their own decisions on how they will live."

He had the good grace to look suitably reprimanded. "You are quite right. I do apologize."

He stood up and paced to his desk, then turned. "However, in my defense, I am of this time and the rules of society are the rules I live by. Although you are independent in your twenty-first century, here you are young and naïve in the eyes of society and, especially, me. *You* must remember, I know you, and despite your brashness, you can quickly become out of your depth. I will try not to be so condescending if you try to behave as if you were born of this time. I am a duke and I have responsibilities to England and our king. And, Elizabeth, I have a responsibility to Alice. There can be no scandal associated with my name. You need to listen to me for all our sakes."

Izzy's shoulders slumped. His aversion to her liking Edward had nothing to do with the fact that she wasn't of this time; it had everything to do with her not being of the noble class. She wasn't good enough.

"Come on," James said, coming to a stop in front of her. "It is not as bad as all that. You have your book to write and once you go home, you will forget about all of us." He held out his arm to her. "It's time to break our fast."

Although she had lost her appetite, Izzy took his arm and walked with him to the dining room, fighting the prickle of tears all the way. Once again, she didn't belong.

The many aromas of a hot breakfast filled Izzy's nose before she stepped through the open door, and despite her disappointment in James and his whole social class, her stomach decided it was hungry after all.

More disappointment besieged her when she realized everyone else must have already had their breakfast, because she and James were alone. He guided her to a chair and sat in his normal place at the head of table.

She accepted the offerings of the footman with what she hoped was good grace and he placed two poached eggs on her plate.

James ate quickly and, plucking up his marmalade toast, said, "I have work to do but the library is all yours."

"Thanks."

Izzy noted his dark frown and tight lips as he left the room. Maybe it was just too much of an imposition to have her there. Her parents probably kept the future hidden. They probably wouldn't have explained how it was for women in the future. James expected her to think and act like women of his day. *Well, that was never going to happen.*

However, Izzy made a silent promise to try hard to at least *seem* like a woman of his time. It shouldn't be so hard. She felt comfortable with most of the rules and mannerisms of the era—she had to admit, she had felt more at home in that time then her own. She tossed the napkin on the table. At least, she had before James reminded her that she didn't belong.

CHAPTER 11

During the following days, every time Izzy and Edward were alone, James found his way to Izzy's side and he would take her somewhere or other. Would you like to go for a ride in my new curricle? Have you seen the blue irises bloom of the season? Come and see the stallion I purchased.

She couldn't deny him even though she knew he was interfering. He thought he was looking after her. It was sweet really. But that morning was different. Izzy wandered into the dining room and James was nowhere to be seen; while Vera and Alice were there, Edward was not.

Trying to hide her disappointment, Izzy smiled at both women. "Good morning."

"Good morning," Alice said.

Vera just nodded.

Izzy gritted her teeth and decided not to take offense. After all, the woman had a mouthful of toast and it would have been impolite to talk with her mouth full. Vera finished eating, stood up, and strode out of the room. She seemed decidedly out of sorts.

Izzy turned to Alice. "Is something wrong?"

Alice smiled widely. "Not at all. Don't mind Vera, she is a little upset that Edward left without asking her to go with him. She is to return to London forthwith."

Izzy didn't care what Vera did. "Edward's left?"

"Yes, he and James have finally come to an arrangement and James is going to introduce Edward to his manager, who has extensive experience in the growing of grape vines. James's manager is French and knows a great deal about wine."

"Oh, so he's going to tell Edward his secrets? That's so... um... nice of him."

Izzy silently slapped herself. She had to be more careful with her words; she was nearly going to say how 'cool' that was.

"James would like nothing better than to have Edward succeed in his new venture. The estates need quite the overhaul."

Izzy put some eggs and toast on her plate. "How long will they be gone?"

"At least two months, I expect."

About to bite into a piece of toast, Izzy's hand stopped dead in front of her mouth. "Two months?"

"Yes, James's manager will be taking them to visit some of the older vineyards to gain an insight into how they go about their farming. And of course, they'll also be learning from the new wineries."

Izzy munched her toast. She guessed it would help Edward a lot to have such knowledgeable people teaching him about his new venture, but Izzy couldn't help but wonder if she'd ever see him again. She had no idea how long she could stay in the past. What if there was some sort of time limit? What if she just vanished back to the future before the men returned?

Izzy frowned at Alice. "I can't believe James didn't speak to me before he left."

"James sends his apologies, but his manager was about to leave the estate this morning when Edward said he would be interested in knowing more about the growing and harvesting of grapes. James made the decision there and then that he and Edward would accompany him."

Izzy bit her bottom lip. *How fortunate.* James got to kill two birds with one stone—spend time with his future stepson and keep Edward from Izzy's company.

She sighed. "I do understand, but I am disappointed that James won't be taking me back to London."

"He spoke to me about that, and I think you will enjoy winter here just as well as London. We will have many entertainments to keep us busy, you will see, and with Vera returning to London, we will have the chance to get to know one another better."

Izzy had to admit she was glad Vera wasn't going to be there the whole time.

OVER THE NEXT TWO MONTHS, IZZY DID INDEED ENJOY HER time in the country. Alice was a wonderful companion and although Izzy hardly had a day to herself, she enjoyed the older woman's company. Alice accepted invitations to balls and dinners. They visited Bath often, attending the upper assembly rooms regularly, and they enjoyed concerts in the Octagon Room.

After nearly two months of being a single woman in 1812, Izzy was quite proud to think she had blended in well with society. No one would have known she didn't belong there. Spring was approaching, and the number of sunny days increased both the warmth and her temperament. However, if she was honest with herself, it wasn't only the sun's rays lifting her spirits; it was the thought that James and Edward would be returning to Chodstone that had her smiling the most.

The day before the men were to return, Alice took Izzy to the last of the winter festivities, an afternoon musicale at the Countess of Fardin's townhouse. Even Alice, who always had a warm disposition, had brightened exponentially upon reading James's missive telling her of their return, and she fairly bounced to the carriage that would take them to Bath.

The snow on the mountains had begun to melt, and the rivulets of water running into the many streams between Chodstone and Bath raised their depths, so that water splashed up from the wheels as they crossed.

Izzy frowned at the sight. "The waters are rising. I hope we can get back."

"It is always like this late winter. The streams run quickly into the sea; we are quite safe."

That made Izzy feel a little better, but even without rain the trickling streams had become raging rivers.

Glad to be off the wet roads and out of the carriage, Izzy settled down to enjoy the musicale. Many notables entertained the guests and wine flowed freely. She was surprised champagne was served. After all, wasn't that why Edward and James wanted to grow grapes? To make up for the loss of French wines?

Lady Fardin was a gracious host, and servants flitted about everywhere with trays of food and bottles of champagne.

During the intermission, Izzy stayed close to Alice, trying to evade the many young gentlemen who had seemingly set their caps for her. One after another, they ventured to speak with Izzy. She was polite but firmly refused their offers of a stroll in the garden or a ride in their new curricles. Knowing how Alice wanted Edward to marry Vera, Izzy was surprised at the woman's reaction when one gentleman wouldn't take no for an answer.

"Miss Davis is already affianced, Lord Brighton," Alice said.

His eyes widened. "I did not know that. Mayhap Miss Davis should have said so earlier."

Alice leaned forward and spoke in a hushed tone. "It is supposed to be a secret, but I know you would not gossip about such a thing."

"No, of course not. Excuse me." He offered a quick bow and hastened to a group of men standing by the wall perusing the room like young lions choosing their prey.

Alice plucked another glass of champagne off a waiter's tray and laughed. "That should keep the hordes from annoying you."

Izzy stared at the woman who had become her friend over the last two months. "Thank you, I think."

Alice drank the wine a little too quickly, to Izzy's mind.

"We both know you cannot make a match. You must return home soon, and I hope I have been useful in making your visit memorable."

"Oh, you have. I have had the best time." Eyeing her friend, Izzy noted the heightened color in her cheeks. "Are you unwell?"

"No. Why do you say so? Do I look unwell?"

Before Izzy could answer, Alice swayed and, holding her hand to her forehead, backed up so that she could sit in a vacant chair. "Mayhap I am a little tired. Bring me a glass of that delightful champagne, please, Elizabeth."

"I think you've had enough wine. We should go home."

"But it's not tomorrow yet."

Izzy had never heard Alice talk such nonsense. "Sorry?"

"I just want to keep busy and entertained until tomorrow."

Izzy grinned. "Because James is coming home?"

Alice blushed like a first-year debutante. "Yes."

"Come on, we had better get you into bed or you won't be in fit state to welcome him home."

Izzy made their excuses to Lady Fardin, saying Lady Wellsneath was feeling a tad under the weather.

Once back in the carriage and hurtling over the first flooded stream, Alice sighed loudly.

"Are you all right?" Izzy asked.

"Yes, yes, I am quite fine. I just wish you were of this time. Then Edward might be persuaded to marry you."

Izzy choked on her surprise. "What?"

"Don't look at me like that. Did you not think James would tell me about you? After all, your parents were my friends also."

"You knew my parents? You knew they were from the future?"

"Did I say that?" She placed her palm on her forehead. "I think the French champagne has gone to my head faster tonight. Mayhap it was a faulty bottle."

"The champagne was fine and yes, you did say that. What do you know of my parents?"

The carriage swayed and Alice groaned. "Please, no more talk. I just want to go to my bed."

"I'm not leaving this alone, Alice. Once we're at Chodstone, I'll make you tea and then you can spill everything."

"Spill the tea? Why?"

"Sorry, it's a saying from where I come from. It means, tell me everything you know."

Alice sat back and closed her eyes.

Once they were back at the house, Izzy asked for a tray to be brought to the front parlor and they were soon sipping tea.

"Here, have a sweet biscuit," Izzy said. "It'll make you feel better."

"I would prefer to go to my bed."

"That's not going to happen just yet, so you may as well drink your tea."

Alice's blue eyes narrowed at Izzy, but she took a bite of a biscuit, swallowed and said, "I am certain there is nothing I can tell you about your parents that you don't know. They were a friendly couple, full of life, and I enjoyed their company immensely."

"When did you last see them?"

"Just after my husband died. That was, in fact, when James confessed the truth about his friends. I'd met them before of course, and always wondered about their strange speech, but James said much the same as he said about you—that they were from America and society there was very different than here. I never had reason not to believe him but something your mother said the last time she and Mark visited gave me pause."

"What did she say?"

"Dianne took my hands in hers and congratulated me on Edward's harvest. Edward walked in then and stood open-mouthed at what he had just heard. I just stared at Dianne and she looked at Edward, saying, *Did you not have a grand harvest?* I said, *He hasn't grown his first vine as yet. How could he have a successful harvest?*"

Alice laughed. "Dianne looked appalled, absolutely appalled, and she stuttered something about mistaking my son for someone else. When I looked at James and Mark, they were standing there with their mouths agape as if they couldn't believe Dianne's words. James was the first to stir and he said, *You have mistaken the earl for the Viscount Comly, Mrs Davis.*" Alice smiled widely. "Then James took me by the hand and led me into the garden and told me all he knew about his friends."

"And you believed him?"

"Not at all, at least not at first. At first I was angry that he would tell me such Banbury tales."

"Huh?"

"Falsehoods. I was certain he was lying to me."

"Of course. But?"

Alice put her cup down and gazed into the distance. "He got to his knees before me and pleaded for me to believe him. The way he looked at me that night, how could I deny him? We agreed we would talk about his revelation after I had time to dwell on his words. We rejoined Mark and Dianne and the night was filled thereafter with revelations of my two new time-traveling friends."

"That must have been a lot to take in."

"It was, but the evidence could not be refuted, and I quite liked the idea of having such friends."

"But you never told Edward."

"No, he would not have believed such a thing, especially if the revelation had come from James's mouth. He detests James."

"Why?"

"That is a long story but suffice to say my marriage was arranged by my father and the earl. My friendship with James at the time was not welcomed. He was, after all, a third son and with no title or lands of his own. I was forced to marry the Earl of Wellsneath." She sighed. "James left for India, where he made his own fortune. I won't say the earl treated me badly, but he never forgave me for loving James."

She gazed off into the distance as if remembering some detail from long ago. "However, the earl doted on the boys and Edward adored his father. He also believed every word the man uttered. His father brought Edward up to think James was a skirt chaser and gambler, of course," she sighed. "The fact that his own father was both those things never seemed to enter Edward's head."

Izzy grinned at Alice and kinked her head sideways. "So, you actually like me."

"Of course, I like you. How could I not? You are intelligent and funny, much like your mother."

"Then why do you do everything you can to keep me and Edward apart?"

"I have seen the way he looks at you and I cannot have him develop a tendre for someone who will leave him. I cannot have his heart broken. Whereas Vera is well-placed in society and a good match in our terms. She will be a good wife and an excellent mother."

Izzy sucked in her bottom lip. "I suppose you're right that he has to have someone of this time, but I'm not sure Vera is the right one. Surely there are other suitable women he could meet?"

"I have been introducing him to society for years and not once has he so much as looked at a woman the way he looks at you. However, he is agreeable to a match with Vera and that is all I ask of him."

Ending the conversation, Alice stood up. "I must retire now."

"Of course." Izzy stood up also. "Good night, Alice."

Once she was gone, Izzy made her way to her own bedroom, but she didn't think she would sleep much that night. She was glad that Alice knew about her, but she was disappointed she still didn't want Izzy getting close to Edward.

His image brought to her mind, excitement welled in her throat. He was to return the next day. No matter what Alice said, in the end it would not be up to her what Edward did. After all, he was the earl and as such ruled his household. She snuggled under the covers. Maybe once he was back, Edward would kiss her again.

CHAPTER 12

Edward and Chodstone, along with the duke's manager, Berkley, had filled their days by touring vineyards and wineries, and with much talk of the same.

But even though he was busy, Edward's thoughts were full of Elizabeth. Her image kept filling his mind at the most inopportune times. What was she doing while he was gone? Where was she going? Whom was she meeting?

He knew his mother intended taking her to as many festivities as she could while the men were away. He wondered if she might develop a tendre for another man in his absence. When his thoughts turned morose, he threw himself into his studies, hoping that the time would pass quickly, and he could return to Chodstone Hall and make his feelings known to Elizabeth before she set her cap elsewhere.

While talking with a reasonably successful landowner in the midst of his vineyard, his manager asked a question. Chodstone deferred to Edward for the answer. Edward knew he was testing him, wanting to see if he had learned anything in all their time away, so he answered as well as he could.

"If you leave more than the main trailer, the vine will not produce as well as it should." Elizabeth's smile filled his mind from out of nowhere. "I... ah." Her eyes seemed to beckon him to her and she lifted her arms as if to take him into an embrace. "I... ah."

"Come, I'll show you," Chodstone said, eyeing Edward as if he had grown two heads.

Edward tried to shake Elizabeth's image out of his head, but her smile filled his chest with warmth and the thought of taking her into his arms had his legs faltering.

He tucked the feelings away to examine at a later time as he followed Chodstone and the estate manager to a row of full-foliaged vines.

Some of the vineyards they visited were doing well, with good production, but others were in need of expertise in growing, pruning, and harvesting. The owners of those vineyards were full of enthusiasm, but their knowledge was grossly inferior to the better producing yards.

The time Chodstone and Berkley spent with the deficient yard owners and managers astounded Edward at first, but after nearly two months in their company, Edward soon came to realize they were a giving duo. No question went unanswered and they gave their knowledge freely without ever expecting anything in return. Edward admired their generosity greatly, even to the point of feeling small-minded at wondering why they were helping what in the long term would be their competitors.

The week before they returned to Chodstone Hall, Edward sat with the duke at a cozy inn in the middle of Dorset. He hadn't asked the duke about his benevolence prior to that night. After all, he himself was a student of the master vine growers and had made copious notes during their wanderings, learning all he could from the other growers' questions and the information Chodstone and Berkley freely gave. However, there was one question Edward wanted to ask, and feeling as if he and Chodstone were becoming fast friends, despite his earlier grievances against the man, he worked up the courage to do so.

"Your Grace?"

The duke put his drink down on the table. "Yes?"

The way Chodstone raised his brows had Edward losing his confidence in the closeness of their friendship, so instead he asked the other thing that was on his mind. "First, I want to thank you and Berkley for including me on this tour. I've learned much and hope to put what I've learned to good use when I get back to Wellsneath."

"I'm glad." Chodstone picked his tankard back up. "And second?"

"I was wondering why you and your manager helped the lesser farms out. That is, why you taught them how to grow and prune the vines when they so clearly will become your competitors. In fact, why you included me, I still have no idea."

"Your last query is an easy answer. I would do anything for your mother, and if she thinks you have it in you to be a great vineyard keeper, then I feel it my duty to teach you all you need to know. Plus Edward, I quite like you, you know." He smiled into his tankard as if waiting for Edward's response.

But Edward didn't say anything. He sat back and studied the man. The Duke of Chodstone was nothing like he had thought. He was a kind, patient man who gave to the poor without a thought and instilled confidence in the people around him. That he had previously dismissed the duke as a skirt chaser and gambler had Edward grimacing with chagrin into his own tankard. The things his father used to say about the duke were so very clearly wrong, mayhap even hatefully vindictive. Oh, he knew his father had been no angel. The man had been himself a womanizer and gambler. That was the reason Edward always believed him so easily. Surely one corrupt man would know another.

"Your main point is a little more complicated," Chodstone continued. "Berkley and I are extremely excited about the burgeoning English wine industry. We believe we will surpass even France's best wines in less than a decade, but to do that we need growers, and not just growers of quantity, but of quality. We need the finest grapes we can grow in our beautifully fertile soils. Vineyards are new to most estate and farm owners. They need instruction on producing top-grade produce and we have the knowledge. Berkley was manager of the largest vineyard in Champagne. He knows all there is to know about cultivating, growing, and harvesting the best grapes and how to best nurture this new industry. We need many fine vineyards producing quality fruit."

Edward was flummoxed that he hadn't seen that himself. Now that the duke put his reasoning into words, it was so clear that Edward was embarrassed about questioning the duke on his rationality.

"That is abundantly understandable now that you explain it. I am an eager student myself and am quite excited to bring my manager and Berkley together." Edward quickly added, "If that is all right with you."

Chodstone held up his tankard to a passing waitress. "Another for myself and my friend."

Her cheeks colored up as she dipped in a curtsy. "Yes, Your Grace."

Watching the waitress hurry to do her lord's bidding, Edward wondered just how well the duke knew the staff at the inn. "You have been here before?"

"I stay here whenever I visit Dorset. It is by far the best inn around, don't you think?"

"It is nice."

The waitress placed two full tankards on the table. "Will that be all, Your Grace?"

"Yes, thank you, Emma."

The way the waitress smiled at the duke as she gave him another curtsy had Edward once more rethinking his previous thoughts. It wasn't a comely smile, it was one filled with respect for the station of the man who had just called her by name.

Sick of small talk, Edward swallowed a mouthful of ale and blurted, "Why do you not think I am a suitable match for Miss Davis?"

"Ah, I've been wondering when you would get around to asking." He drank more ale, then chuckled. "Why do you think it is so?"

"I thought at first it was because you didn't like me, but you said yourself you did." Edward rubbed his chin. "However, now I am inclined to believe Vera and see you want her for yourself."

Chodstone laughed and slammed his hand on the table as if to get himself under control. Everyone in the inn stared at him but as he quieted his mirth, they all went back to their drinking, eating, and chatting.

"Have you not noticed my attentions to your mother?"

"Being a man, I can see how you could enjoy my mother's company. But a woman like Elizabeth is rare and you are always in her company. Even an honorable gentleman would find it difficult to keep his thoughts from going astray where she is concerned."

Chodstone narrowed his eyes at Edward, piercing him with his now deep brown eyes. "You besmirch my honor? You think I would have a young innocent in my house and not see her as the daughter I never had?" He sat back with a sigh. "She is that, you know. Though she is the daughter of close friends, the moment she stepped into my home as my ward, she became a daughter to me. How dare you call me out on such a thing? Have you no honor yourself?"

Edward didn't know what to say. Everything he had seen in the last two months told him the man was indeed most honorable, but he did have Izzy in his arms that night. He eyed Chodstone. The way the duke stroked his chin and glared at him had Edward choosing his words carefully. He did not want to cause a ruckus at the inn. After all, many patrons were known to the duke and the gossips would wag their tongues all the way to London town. However, he did not like to be spoken to in such a manner, especially after what he had seen with his own eyes.

Edward folded his arms across his chest and glared back at Chodstone. "I saw you holding Elizabeth in your arms the night of the dinner at Wellsneath."

The duke frowned and looked over Edward's shoulder for a moment. Returning his gaze to Edward, a spark appeared in his now calm brown eyes and he smiled. "Yes, I remember." He leaned forward as if to tell Edward a great conspiracy. "Do you want to know why?"

Edward kept his arms folded. "Yes."

He shrugged. "I told her Alice and I were to be married."

Edward drew in a sharp intake of breath, but Chodstone continued.

"Elizabeth was happy for me and hugging me like that was the way she chose to show it. Now what do you say to that?"

Relief flooded through Edward. Chodstone and Elizabeth were not affianced. He gave an imperceptible shake of his head, feeling silly for believing such a thing. Surely, she would not have kissed him if she were already spoken for? Edward schooled his face. He didn't want the duke knowing how his words comforted him. He kept his voice low, so their neighbors could not hear him. "You are to marry my mother?"

"Yes."

"Why is it a secret?"

"Your mother wanted to see you settled first."

"Me? To Vera, I suppose?"

"Yes."

"So that is why she has been pushing the match so earnestly. I imagine if she thought I was settled, she could do anything she wanted."

"That is part of it, I'm sure, but your mother only wants what is best for you. Vera is a good match, isn't she?"

"She would be to some noble, I'm certain of it, but me? I am unsure if we are suited."

"Please do not have thoughts of Elizabeth. She will be departing soon and we might never see her again. She did say something about being engaged before she left America."

"To whom?"

"I do not know."

"You are her protector and you don't know whom she is to marry?" Edward shook his head. "If she was to be married, why did she come here then?"

"There are reasons, Edward, and I am in no position to reveal them."

CHAPTER 13

Edward entered Chodstone Hall's second reception room in the hope that he could spend some time alone with Elizabeth that afternoon but soon found that impossible. She was ensconced in a game of whist with Vera and Alice.

Elizabeth had just won another game, and Vera said, "If I didn't know Miss Davis and her handsome guardian, I would think she was cheating." She laughed. "But of course, I do know you and would never think such a thing for certainty. But tell me, darling, how do you play so well?"

She smiled at Chodstone. "His Grace taught me well, I suppose."

"She is a quick study and I am most fortunate to have such a wonderful player to keep me on my toes, am I not?"

"Yes, indeed, Your Grace."

Vera said the words with a smile, but Edward saw the resentment in her eyes as her gaze landed on Elizabeth.

Edward's mother stood up. "And I am the worst card player in all of England. Come along, Miss Davis, I would like your opinion of some fabric I purchased this morning."

Once they'd left, Chodstone took his leave also and, not wanting to be alone with Vera, Edward left for Wellsneath without so much as a word to her.

THAT EVENING, EDWARD WAS BACK AT CHODSTONE HALL and about to dine with Elizabeth. He paced the foyer, but the movement didn't help Edward's mood one iota. Since the night in the maze, the night he had kissed Elizabeth, she had been all he could think about. Her warmth, her attraction to him, he almost growled aloud his attraction to her. He had never felt that way before. He'd had many dalliances, but no woman had ever touched his heart, his soul, like she had.

She was different indeed, and although something in the back of his mind warned him not to become too close, that there was something strongly different about her, his foremind and his body liked the differences, liked her way of speech, liked her.

Keep pacing.

He had thought to rid himself of the need to see Elizabeth—the incessant need to be alone with her. After two whole months without her company, one would expect his longing to have declined but during that time all he could do was think about her, think about holding her in his arms and not letting her go for all time. Even when intrigued with the art of growing grapes and the alchemy of turning those grapes into wine, Elizabeth's smiling image would appear in his mind and he would stop listening to his tutors.

Keep pacing.

He had to know if it was true, if she was to be married to some unknown American. He thought the forced movement would rid himself of his irritability and his restlessness before he joined his host and the other guests for dinner.

Mayhap if he talked with Elizabeth, learned more about her, the silly notion of a goddess walking amongst them would dispel. Life could then return to its normal, predictable routine. He could go on as he had before that fateful night when his carriage nearly ran her down.

He had hoped to do just that that afternoon, but the duke and his mother kept Elizabeth and Vera busy playing whist. He let out a gust of air. Vera had been most ungracious to her host's ward. Chodstone didn't seem to discern her insults, but Edward could, and if he were Elizabeth's guardian, he would not put up with Vera's abuse of her character a moment longer.

He spun on his heels and strode to the front door.

Keep pacing.

He turned to retrace his steps once more but stopped abruptly as Elizabeth descended the stairs. He knew he was staring—no, ogling—but he couldn't help himself. She was beautiful. He drank her in from foot to head, from the blue slippers peeking out from the sapphire-blue gown that fell like a steady stream meandering over the contours of her body from its source under her bust. Her sun-kissed skin darkened slightly toward her neck. Her small chin dimpled as her pink lips widened in a smile.

He couldn't find the sense to smile back. He knew he still stared.

If he hadn't been watching her so closely, he would have missed her slight hesitation at his dark look. Had she seen the lust in his eyes or had his previous irritability shown itself?

Nevertheless, she continued down the stairs and once she silently stepped in front of him, she bobbed in a quick curtsy. "My lord."

"Please call me Edward."

She gazed up to him through her dark lashes, a small mischievous smile playing on her lips. "Edward."

It was all he could do not to take her in his arms and kiss the mischief out of her and replace it with passion. Passion he could feel emanating from her.

"I apologize for staring, but you are a beautiful sight."

"Thank you." Her lips widened into a beaming smile, her teeth once again impressing him with their whiteness. "So are you."

He laughed. "Thank you." His face suddenly turned serious. "I must also apologize for Vera's rudeness to you this afternoon."

"Don't worry about it. She's probably jealous, which is understandable, you know. You probably shouldn't look at me quite so much. Especially when you are to marry her."

"So my mother would have you believe, but I haven't decided when I will be married or even if I ever will be."

"Oh?"

Her blue eyes sparkled with curiosity, but dark desire tinted them as she gazed at his mouth. Was she remembering that kiss, that wonderfully marvelous kiss? The tip of her pink tongue flicked out to wet her lips. He had to forcibly hold his arms at his sides so as not to crush her against him and taste her once more.

"What about you? Chodstone told me you were affianced in America. Is that true?"

"Um..." Sadness now tinged those same blue eyes, chasing the sparkle from them. "I don't think so."

Had he heard correctly? Mayhap the engagement was broken. "You don't think you are engaged to be married?" He tried to sound encouraging, wanting her to expand on what she had said, but afraid to hear how she loved another.

"I don't want to talk about it."

His body leaned in toward her of its own volition and his

heart hammered in his chest when she mirrored his movement. He lowered his head, keeping his eyes pinned on the target that was her lips. Those same lips opened and again she licked her top lip.

But then, she hesitated. Thinking she was about to reject him, he pulled back. They both stood there looking everywhere but at one another in awkward silence.

What was he doing? She was unavailable, and he had to keep his wits about him or he would end up ruining her. He drew his brows together at the thought that if he did ruin her, would the duke insist he do the honorable thing and marry her? If it were anyone else that would be the case, but Elizabeth was different. Something told him Chodstone might not demand marriage, and Edward wanted to know why.

He caught sight of his mother and the duke out of the corner of his eye. He combed his fingers through his hair as his eyes met his mother's curious gaze.

"There you are," she said as if she had misplaced him.

"Mother." He tipped his head in a small bow to Chodstone, who held out his arm to Elizabeth with what Edward could only think was a command, by the hard look he gave Elizabeth.

The moment she placed her hand on his forearm, the duke hurried her into the dining room. Once she was out of sight, Edward turned to his mother.

His mother didn't move; she just stood there. Her regard of him had him straightening his waist coat with one hand and pulling on his cravat with the other. He thought she seemed to be choosing her words—too carefully for his liking.

"Edward, you must restrain yourself. Miss Davis isn't like the town women you usually find in your company. And although she may be older than a first-year debutante, she is an innocent and she is the duke's ward. I expect you to treat her as such. We don't need a scandal and I'm sure James would prefer not to be involved in one."

Edward didn't care two hoots about Chodstone or his reputation, but he did care about Elizabeth, err, Miss Davis. And although he wouldn't say so, he agreed with his mother. Elizabeth deserved someone better than him, but he couldn't abide thinking of her stuck in a marriage with someone she wasn't even sure of. He peered at his mother. If she didn't know about the relationship between the unknown American and Elizabeth, what exactly was her argument against him pursuing a relationship with her? Was she such a snob that she didn't think Elizabeth was up to the mark?

"Now Edward, I know you too well and your thoughts are clear to me. You think I don't approve of Miss Davis, don't you?"

Edward raised his brows and tipped his head to the side.

"That isn't it at all. I think she would make a perfectly respectable wife to any titled gentleman. It's just that she isn't the right one for you. Vera is and that's all I'm going to say on the subject."

She indicated he should hold his arm out for her. When he did, she placed her hand on his forearm.

"Goodness, what would Vera think of you alone in the foyer with a pretty young woman? She would be aggravated. Your match with her is all but announced."

"Mother, I have decided not to offer for Vera."

"What? What are you thinking, Edward? It is already settled. The only thing to decide is the date of the wedding and then the banns can go out."

"Mayhap you and Vera have settled it, but I have not been consulted in any meaningful way. I find I have few feelings for Vera. I also think it would be better for Vera to find a more suitable match."

"Of course, you're worried about the marriage state. It is

natural after all. However, Vera is willing to wait until you realize it would be the honorable thing to do. You are a gentleman and you will act like one. You also have a title to think about and you need an heir. She is perfect, and you know it."

CHAPTER 14

J ames showed Izzy to her seat at the dining table. The vicar, Mr Hammond, and his wife were already seated. The Vicar stood up and bowed and Mrs Hammond, although in deep conversation with Vera, lifted her eyes at her husband's movement and smiled at Izzy. Vera ignored Izzy completely and continued her conversation with Mrs Hammond.

Izzy fought not to roll her eyes at Vera like a twelve-year-old as Edward and Alice approached the table. The poor vicar was almost seated again when he and James stood up and bowed to Alice.

Alice smiled at the rest of the guests, her eyes lingering on James. "I am sorry to keep you waiting." She waved her hand at Mr Hammond. "Please, Mr Hammond, sit and enjoy your meal."

James sat next to the vicar and opposite Elizabeth, ignoring the fact that Vera had moved the chair next to her out a little for him. Izzy gave the table a wide smile and settled that smile on Edward. She would have liked to continue their conversation in the foyer, but Alice and James seemed to be in agreement that she and Edward shouldn't be left alone.

Knowing Alice had known her parents and where she herself came from, made Izzy feel a little better about being watched so closely. It wasn't that Alice disliked Izzy; she just didn't think it right for Edward to be involved with someone who would return to the future. And, Izzy supposed, neither Alice nor James wanted Edward to know the truth. She glanced at Edward. What would he say to the truth?

Izzy touched her napkin to her lips. She could have sworn he was going to kiss her again in the foyer and she couldn't believe how disappointed she was that he hadn't. Had he changed his mind, or had he heard James and Alice approaching? Izzy was so mind-fuddled, she wouldn't have heard anything even if they had been wearing army boots and not soft-soled shoes and slippers.

Every time someone asked Izzy a question, Vera narrowed her eyes, and the moment Izzy took a breath during the answering of said question, the horrid woman would butt in and give her own answer.

James asked Izzy, "Do you like to ride?"

"I do. In fact, the last time I rode I raced my brother. Our horses were both equally fast and Garrett and I were head to head..."

She took a breath and just as she was about to say who won, Vera piped in, "I love to ride, especially in a hunt."

Izzy cast her attention to her plate. She didn't want to hear about Lady Crompton's penchant for riding down little foxes. She couldn't help it if her face showed how much she detested the thought of chasing a small animal with large dogs and horses.

Vera stared at Izzy as if she couldn't believe what she was seeing. "You do not like to hunt?"

"I hate the thought of it. I can't help but feel sorry for the fox," Izzy said. "The noise of dogs barking, the horse's hooves beating the ground, and horns blasting must scare the poor little thing senseless."

Vera laughed. She actually laughed. "The best foxes escape to be hunted another day." She then went on, telling a story about one such fox.

"I have witnessed you riding the hunt," Mrs Hammond said, "and I must say, you seat a horse perfectly."

Vera beamed at the woman. "I thank you, Mrs Hammond."

Mrs Hammond touched her napkin to the corners of her mouth. "Lady Crompton, my husband and I would be honored if you would agree to cut the ribbon at the opening of the new vicarage."

Vera straightened her back with an air of self-importance. "Thank you. I would love to be included in the ceremony."

"And," Mrs Hammond continued, "Lord Wellsneath, we would be doubly honored if you would agree to accompany your fiancée."

Edward choked on his mouthful of spring lamb. "Fiancée? I'm sorry, but there seems to be a misunderstanding. I have no fiancée."

Mrs Hammond covered her mouth with her napkin. "I apologize, my lord, I thought..." she glanced at Vera. "I thought..."

"Now, now, Wellsneath," Vera crooned. "Don't make Mrs Hammond uncomfortable. The banns are not out at this time, but they will be by the vicarage's opening, will they not?" She gazed at Alice.

Alice cleared her throat. "I think this is a conversation for another time," she stated firmly. "I do hope you are enjoying your meal, Mrs Hammond."

"I am, thank you."

Izzy could almost taste the relief flowing from the vicar's

wife. Vera had obviously told Mrs Hammond of her and Edward's engagement, but it seemed to Izzy, Edward did not know about it. Izzy knew it shouldn't, but Edward's stunned renunciation of Mrs Hammond's statement warmed her chest. Her gaze drifted from Lady Crompton to Lord Wellsneath. Vera appeared to be certain of the banns going out in the near future, so why would Edward be surprised by it all?

"Lady Crompton?" James said when she was finished. "Have you seen the latest French fashions? I see that puffed sleeves are once again popular and a heart-shaped neckline is attractive, is it not?"

Glad for the change of subject, Izzy glanced at Edward, who was watching her with obvious interest. Vera mentioned the lowness of the necklines that season and Edward's gaze washed over Izzy's décolletage; not that hers was low, but any skin showing in that time felt excessive, and his glance burned.

Heat rushed into Izzy's cheeks and she flitted her eyes around the room, hoping no one else had noticed his look. But she could tell by Vera's hostile stare that she, for one, had noticed. Thankfully, however, James and Alice were talking to the vicar, and Mrs Hammond seemed intent on eating every crumb of blueberry pie on her plate.

Vera sipped her wine, regarding Izzy through narrowed eyes. "Alice tells me you write, Miss Davis."

The dragon made the word 'write' sound as if it were something dragged up out of a toilet. Something told Izzy she was about to be set up and her answer came out slowly. "Yes."

"Do you play an instrument? The harpsichord, for instance?"

"No." Again, she answered slowly and picked up her glass of wine. She figured she would need the fortification.

"Do you draw?"

Ah, a quicker answer came to her. "No, but my brother is a marvelous painter. He can paint anything."

"It seems you lack the talents ladies need today. Mayhap we can guide you in your studies. Alice is an accomplished pianist, and I have some skill in playing and singing. Ah, mayhap you sing?"

Yeah, along with the radio. "No. I wouldn't torture anyone with my singing voice. However, I would love to hear you sometime." She smiled and tried to make it appear heartfelt.

"You have the voice of an angel," Mrs Hammond said to Vera. "I too would love to hear you again."

Alice joined the conversation at that moment. "What a wonderful idea. We will stage a recital. Edward can play while Vera sings and I will play for James. He has a beautiful voice. Mrs Hammond, I am told your daughter has studied violin in Italy, is that correct?"

Mrs Hammond's face filled with pride. "She has and would be honored to be invited to play at your recital."

"There," Vera said. "Even the vicar's daughter has talent." She sat back, giving Izzy a pointed look, as if that proved Izzy was less than a lady.

Izzy glanced at Alice but noted that Edward's mother had missed Vera's rudeness.

"Miss Davis is a most accomplished writer by all counts," Edward said.

"But writing is man's work," Mrs Hammond said. "It's not something in which a lady should indulge."

The woman either didn't see or ignored Edward's deathly stare.

"What about Mrs Radcliffe?" James said, trying to help.

Vera's usually staid expression twisted into a sneer as she let out a laugh. "I have heard from a most reliable source, Mrs Radcliffe is a man."

Izzy laid her napkin on the table. "She is indeed a woman.

Ann Radcliffe, born Ann Ward in Holborn, July 9, 1764. She married William Radcliffe in Bath in 1788. She—"

Vera huffed noisily and waved her hand around to stop Izzy continuing with her speech.

"I believe you, but that's enough about the destroyer of young minds."

Edward threw his napkin on his plate. "Lady Crompton, you are being extremely rude. I feel you should apologize to Miss Davis."

"Now Edward," Alice said. "Vera is allowed to air her opinions on such matters."

"What matters are they, Mother?"

"Why matters that concern ladies, of course," Vera said smugly at Alice coming to her defense. "You know nothing of what ladies have to deal with, Edward. We must hold true to society's expectations at all times."

"She is correct," Alice said, and Mrs Hammond nodded in agreement.

Edward pushed his chair back with a scrape, shot both women black glares, and stormed out of the room.

James indicated to a footman to continue serving. The air was heavy with tension as the poor man set two platters of cheeses, dried fruit, and small cakes in the center of the table.

Izzy stared at the last course while Mrs Hammond attacked it with her fork as if she were starving. The vicar seemed to enjoy the small cakes while Alice chose to nibble on a dried fruit. James chose not to eat anything.

Feeling bad about the tension, Izzy chose what she thought looked like a dried fig, but upon taking a bite, it stuck in her throat. She washed it down with some wine, wishing the meal would end. She bit her lip. Edward and his mother's relationship seemed strained. And it was all her fault. When she had first met them, they were lovingly free in one another's company.

She shouldn't have let Vera get to her. After all, the woman was to be Edward's wife, and Alice must have liked her a lot to come to her defense the way she did.

Izzy tried to take another bite of the sweet fruit. She was the interloper. *I don't belong in this time—I don't belong with these people.*

⚜

IZZY WAS UP AND DRESSED EARLY THE NEXT MORNING. SHE didn't like to write until the sun filled her bedroom with light, and it being only seven o'clock, she decided she needed to walk off some unexpended energy. Being a lady in the early nineteenth century had one being almost immobile. Sitting around receiving guests for tea, sewing samplers, playing instruments: none of that made for a strong constitution.

She made her way to the back parlor and quickly threaded her way through the settees, uncomfortable chairs, and small tables already boasting vases of freshly cut flowers. Maybe being a servant in these times was better for one's health—at least, a servant of the gentry. They at least got some exercise.

Throwing the doors wide open, Izzy caught her breath at the chill in the air. Thankful she had grabbed her thick coat, she stepped out onto the patio. Quickly putting it on, she gazed at the vista before her.

The sun was peeking through the gray clouds and its light was falling beside the perfectly kept flower garden. She hurried down the stairs and, to keep her blood warm, walked briskly over the damp path toward the beautifully perfumed daphne and sarcococca shrubs. But it was the sight of the low gardens planted with irises, white cyclamens, and snowdrops that she wanted to take delight in.

Once there, she enjoyed the slight warmth of the sun's rays, and gazed at the many blue, pink, and white flowers.

Breathing in the scent of the flowering shrubs, and letting her shoulders fall in relaxation, she dawdled around the centre pond, reveling in the display. It wasn't long before she found herself at the end of the garden and she let out a snort. This wasn't going to exercise her mushy muscles.

She headed out beyond the garden and walked swiftly down the oak-lined esplanade that wound around the lake. She'd only gone a few steps when footsteps crunched the gravel behind her. Who else would be out there that time of day? She spun around.

Her breath caught in her throat, and her heart somersaulted at the sight of Edward hurrying toward her.

Once he was beside her, he tilted his head to indicate they should walk. She did, and he breathed hard as if he were out of breath, but Izzy guessed he was just pretending.

"I saw you leave the house and followed you. I hadn't thought you could walk so fast. You have me quite out of breath."

"I took my time in the winter garden and wasn't walking that fast anyway. Perhaps you're out of condition."

An appalled look spread over his face. "You wound me, Miss Davis."

"I doubt that, my lord." Izzy let out a laugh but quickly looked around. "We shouldn't be alone, should we?"

"It is not improper when we have so many witnesses. He pointed to the large glass doors of the dining room and many windows on that side of the house, then flicked his head to the right.

Izzy gazed through the trees. The gardeners were out in force. Some trimmed the high hedges on the other side of the green, while others scythed the grass closer to the house, where the sheep that kept the lawns down elsewhere on the estate weren't allowed to roam.

Feeling reassured, Izzy looked up at Edward through her

lashes. His profile was relaxed, and he seemed in good humor, but the small tic in his slightly tightened jaw told her he wasn't completely at ease.

"I must apologize for last evening," Izzy said. "I didn't mean to cause a scene."

"You have nothing to apologize for. Lady Crompton should extend her apologies to all. I question my mother's assumption that Lady Crompton and I do indeed make a suitable match." He gave his head a quick shake. "Please, think no more of it."

He was probably sorry he'd said anything against Vera, but Izzy couldn't help a feeling of elation at his confession. Of course, she had no right to feel that way. He was of a different time and marriages in these times were rarely love matches. They were arranged for the benefit of the family's standing, and heirs were the most important product of a marriage.

She looked around. Even so, she wished they weren't so conspicuous. She gazed at his lips. How she wanted those lips on hers again. He cocked his head, piercing her eyes with his.

Heat filled Izzy's cheeks. Had he seen her thoughts on her face?

He glanced at the house and set his jaw in a tight line with that same little tic. "I think it is time we return to the house and the breakfast table."

Izzy followed his gaze and noted James stepping out of the dining room doors onto the patio. Her guardian was never far away when Edward was around. Izzy sighed. She wanted to spend more time with Edward, but it was time to pretend to be a lady again.

CHAPTER 15

Edward watched James teach Elizabeth piquet. She had only had instruction for three games and already she was settling into the rhythm of the game.

Vera swept into the front parlor, dragging her son, Michael, alongside her. "Edward, it is such a lovely day, I have organized Cook to make a picnic hamper for us. The footmen are waiting in the back garden."

Irritation surged through him at her command.

"Please, my lord?"

He chased the irritation away with a smile at Michael. Edward glanced at his mother, hoping for respite, but Vera wasn't going to take no for an answer.

She looked at Alice. "You don't mind do you, Alice?"

Alice looked up from her sewing. "It sounds wonderful and it is such a lovely day for a picnic," Alice said, smiling fondly at Michael. "I'm sorry I hadn't thought of it."

Glaring at her, Edward said, "Would you like to join us, then?"

133

She shook her head, "No, Lady Farrington and her daughters are coming for tea this afternoon."

"Miss Davis? Would you like to join us?"

Her blue eyes widened, and he was sure she was about to agree, but Vera cut in before she could open her mouth.

"Cook has only prepared enough for two." And as if she had just remembered her son, she looked at him and added. "And a half."

She scooped Edward's arm up in hers.

Irritated by her manipulations but sorry for Michael, he felt like a landed fish with her hook firmly embedded in his mouth. His mother was watching, and he couldn't embarrass the countess with the truth of his thoughts, so he let Michael tug him to the door.

Glancing back at Elizabeth with a chagrined look, Edward left with Vera and Michael.

A footman carrying a blanket and a large basket that Edward thought could hold a meal for half a dozen hungry people waited for them on the pathway that would take them to the esplanade.

Vera stepped toward the footman but stopped and turned to peer over the gate that led to the walled garden. "Oh, look, Michael, the crocuses are flowering. Let's make our picnic there."

Although the child was present, Edward wasn't happy about being alone with Vera. But without waiting for Edward's acquiescence, she urged Michael into the garden and waved the footman ahead.

After they had eaten their full, and with a glass of wine in hand, Edward relaxed back on one elbow as he watched Michael chase butterflies.

Vera's voice broke into his thoughts and suddenly, he wished it was Elizabeth's words enveloping him instead of Vera's caustic tongue.

"Miss Davis seems out of sorts here, doesn't she?"

"I think she fits very well." At least she would if Edward ever had the chance to take her measure.

"I can't see what James sees in her. Even if she is an heiress." She leaned closer to Edward's ear. "That's what James said when I asked about her standing in America, but I think she is wholly unsuited for life in the *ton*."

"Whether she is an heiress or not does not signify—she is Chodstone's ward and as such deserves to be treated with respect."

"But you have to agree she is uneducated in the ways of the gentry. She doesn't even know what being a duchess entails. How can she think to embarrass the duke like that? He and she will be the target of malicious tongues."

Edward sat up, placed his glass on the blanket to stop from throwing it at the woman, and drilled her with his gaze.

"The duke and Miss Davis are not affianced, and you would do well to put a halt to that rumor. I will thank you to not malign Miss Davis's character further. It is unseemly."

"And I will thank you not to speak to me in that way. Your manners leave much to be desired. Tell me, Edward, are you taken with her too?"

Ignoring her, he stood up, caught Michael as he raced past, and placed the boy on the ground before him. "Would you like to swing?"

"Yes please."

Vera huffed and tapped the boy on his leg with her fan.

Michael's smile fell from his face. "My lord."

"We are family, Michael. You do not have to call me 'my lord' when we're alone." He held out his hands. "What is my name?"

Michael jumped up into his arms. "Edward."

"Good. Now hop on the swing and I'll push you."

Michael scrambled onto the wooden plank and held tight to the ropes. "Right up to the sky?"

"Right up to the sky."

Vera left the blanket and joined them at the swing.

"Higher," Michael roared.

"That's high enough," Vera said, more to Edward than to Michael. "Are you planning to befriend Miss Davis more than you have already?"

Edward kept pushing Michael, who was yelling out in glee.

"I saw you kiss her the other night. It would hurt your mother to see such familiarity."

Edward pushed a little too hard and Michael wailed. "You nearly pushed me off, Edward."

"My apologies, young sir."

Vera's words had pierced Edward's heart. He would not intentionally do anything that would hurt his mother. She had been hurt enough in this life; she deserved peace now.

He reined in his anger and he pushed against the child's back more gently. Glancing at Vera, he caught his muscles bunching, and before he shoved Michael right off the swing, he straightened and let the boy's swing sway back and forth under its own momentum.

Her self-satisfied look told him she had gotten the reaction she was looking for. He thought back on that night. The way she appeared without warning had him wondering if she had indeed witnessed that act. Her dislike for Elizabeth seemed to grow after then.

"Mayhap you are mistaken in what you saw."

"I know what I saw and, if you are wondering why I didn't call you out, you must know I am in complete agreement with your mother that we make a perfectly suitable match. I know the ways of the *ton* and you cannot deny I would make an exceptional countess."

"I haven't made up my mind." He had made up his mind of course. He planned to spend every available moment with Miss Elizabeth Davis, and if by any chance they were alone, he would steal another kiss. He wanted more but he would not ruin the girl. A thought flashed in his head. Mayhap he could marry her, though.

"That's enough for today, Michael."

The child pouted and grumbled, but at Vera's cutting aspect, he stopped and said, "Thank you, Edward."

The poor boy needed someone to champion his cause and, just like his brother, Edward had been more than willing to be that person—until he met the strange Miss Davis on a cold night where she wore nothing but a day dress and light pelisse. The moment his skin touched hers as he helped her onto her feet, a thrilling tickle scuttled through his body. And when his eyes met her worried blue orbs, the tickle became a throb deep down in his gut and if he hadn't taken his hands off her in that second, he would have ravished her there and then in the middle of Fleet Street.

Vera gave Michael a little shove. "Run ahead, darling." Turning to Edward, she said, "You cannot let your mother down like that, Edward. To make a match with someone of her standing, or should I say, lack of standing. She would pollute your bloodline and your mother would be miserable for all her days."

Keeping his mouth tightly shut so he wouldn't say something he would come to regret, Edward stared off over the low wall. Even in his anger, he knew she was right. He was honor-bound to comply with his mother's wishes. His heart broke a little at that and he wasn't prepared for the pain. He humphed.

"I'll leave you to think about what I have said." And with that, Vera grabbed her son's hand and strutted out of the garden, apparently pleased with the way the conversation had gone.

Edward strode out of the formal garden and walked across the field, kicking dried cow patties as he went. Why had he gone there? He had thought if he got to know Elizabeth more deeply, he would see it was his imagination that had elevated her in his thoughts. The night he met her—well, almost killed her—he was tired of the daughters of ambitious mamas. Tired of the *ton* and their gossips. Tired of his title and all that came with it. Tired of having his future planned for him. Oh, he knew he would never have a love match, but he was tired of Vera and all she stood for.

Bending down, he picked a pink cowslip and without thinking brought it to his nose. It reminded him of Elizabeth with its light, innocent apricot scent. He had smelt a similar fragrance about her when he first met her, that and something exclusively her. He sniffed the flower. How he wanted to smell Elizabeth again.

He threw the flower aside. Elizabeth would return to America. Why had she come to England? Why didn't she know if she had a fiancé or not? Why was Chodstone so set against them getting to know one another better? So many questions. He should have stayed in London as he had planned. He should have busied himself with the plans for his estate and immersed himself in politics, both of which were uncomplicated and predictable.

CHAPTER 16

Edward had gone to Wellsneath to sort out the planting of the grape vines. James had offered to help him, but Edward declined, saying he had already taken too much of James's time.

The last thing Izzy wanted was to be cooped up with Vera all day, so when Alice suggested a shopping trip, Izzy begged off, complaining of a headache.

Happy to have some time to herself, Izzy settled down to continue writing her book. She conjured up a picture of her sister and her Scottish husband. The way they looked at one another made Izzy's heart heavy. Would she ever have someone look at her with not just love but admiration and respect? She grinned and let out a snort. They always seemed a breath away from ripping one another's clothes off.

Izzy wondered why she felt a tinge of jealousy at that thought. She had never wanted to rip anyone's clothes off and she sure as hell didn't want anyone taking such liberties with her person. She smiled at the turns of phrase flying through her head. She was getting used to the nineteenth century's way of speaking. She was also getting used to seeing Edward every day.

Her disappointment at him not being at breakfast that morning cut through her as painfully as a physical knife wound. She shook her head and tried to concentrate on her writings. He was out of her reach. He was committed to Vera and would make a fine father for her son. She had no place daydreaming about him looking at her like Iain looked at Abby.

Abby's love story was the thing of dreams, a once in a life-time deal.

She picked up her papers and began reading. What had she been thinking? The setting had changed from Scotland to England. The all-too-proper laird seemed very like a handsome earl she knew and the heroine, small and petite like her, not tall and elegant like Abby. The story was full of her very real emotions, not her imaginings of how Abby felt.

She should have been more in control of her feelings from the moment she met the man. The tingling at his touch when he helped her onto her feet should have warned her he was dangerous. She frowned down at the page. But how could it? She had never before felt such a thing. No one had ever engendered such a reaction, such a primal longing to have him touch her again.

Her finger brushed her lips. She could still feel the pres-sure of his lips against hers, the teasing of his tongue asking for an invitation to enter, and her eager response. She had become completely lost in the moment, in the surprising but enjoyable sensations that coursed through her body. No, she could never have envisioned having to protect herself from such a state. She sighed. Edward. No man had spawned such reactions; her body had usurped her mind and taken complete control. And had there been more time, she would have willingly and so freely let him take her, ravish her until they were altogether spent.

She dropped her head into her hands and groaned. Even now, her body was betraying her. Just the thought of the Earl of Wellsneath had her breathless.

She gazed at the title. *The Laird and his Lady*. Letting out a huff, she picked up the pen and scratched the title out, replacing it with a new title. *The Duke and the Dairy Maid*.

She snorted. "That's just silly."

However, she couldn't help but wonder why she chose "Dairy Maid" and not something like "Duchess." Maybe it was because that was where she fit best. She didn't belong in the aristocracy. Elizabeth Davis could never be a duchess. Edward's image filled her mind. Or a countess.

Sure, she had a reasonable standing as a writer in her time, however tenuous that was. But she always felt a bit of a fraud. When her series was chosen for television, she kept wondering when they would realize it wasn't good enough to invest so much money in. She sighed. If only she could keep busy like she had then, then she wouldn't have time to inspect her faults, she wouldn't have time to see how she didn't fit in to English society even more than she didn't fit in the twenty-first century.

Even if she were from that time period, even if she really were an American heiress, there was no way she could fit in. Vera was right; Izzy was a country bumpkin compared to her. Tears prickled the back of her eyes and she tried to blink them away. No point crying about it. She had no right to turn up there and mess with people's lives. No matter how much her treacherous body or her dull-witted mind was drawn to Edward, no matter how much she wanted to bed the man. There, she said it. Well, thought it anyway. She wanted to make love to Edward, and she didn't care if she was married to the man or not.

If there was anyone in the whole world or in any time period whom she wanted to give herself to, it was Edward. It was Edward with whom she wanted to soar to those raging heights she had only read about. Oh, how she wanted to experience the closeness of being with someone she loved, being united in body and soul.

Snorting again, she shook her head and wiped the first tears from her cheeks. She sniffed. Maybe she was right to hold out for her perfect man. Maybe there was someone like Edward in her time, someone she could feel the same primal lust for. She hadn't thought it possible to feel any of those things but now, she knew, she would definitely be on the lookout for that tingling of excitement shooting through her body.

Oh, how she wanted to feel all that, again and again.

She pushed hard against the small desk, scraping her chair back, and stood up.

There was only one thing for it. She had to leave Chodstone Hall and leave Edward to live his life as he would have done before she fell out of the sky.

She paced to the bed and back.

Yes, she would leave—go to London, finish her book, and then return home.

❦

Izzy couldn't shut herself in her room any longer; she had to find James. She found him in his study, his usual late morning space.

"James?"

He looked up from his desk, and while she noted a slight annoyance on his brow as he pushed his papers aside, he smiled. "Elizabeth. Please come in."

Standing up and pulling the bell, he indicated Izzy should sit. "Tea?"

She nodded and chose the settee near the fire. Tea was something she had never had much of in her time. Compared to coffee, it was bland, but she wondered now if it was as addictive as coffee because she had gotten quite a taste for it —and those little cakes James's cook always served were to die for.

James sat in the chair on the side of the low table opposite Izzy.

"To what do I owe this pleasure?"

"I've been thinking I should go back to London."

He thought about that for a moment. "And why is that?"

"I'm at a part in my book that needs me to see London's way of life. I need to shop and go to balls and such so I can get a feel of the places and the people."

"And to get away from Wellsneath?"

Heat once again rose in her face. She bit the inside of her cheek. She hated blushing like a schoolgirl every time Edward's name was mentioned. In truth it wasn't his name that caused her embarrassment, it was where her mind went at the mention of him. Her lips tingled with passion, as if he'd just kissed her there and then.

As if he could read her mind, James pierced her with a look. Thankfully, a knock at the door heralded their tea.

Once the butler had departed, Izzy poured the tea while James watched her with intense eyes.

He accepted his teacup. "I think it a marvelous idea. Are you ready to leave now?"

Izzy nodded. "I've already packed, but would you be coming with me?"

"I cannot leave my houseguests, but I will send a footman and your abigail with you." He stood up and went to his desk, pulled out a sheet of paper, and wrote something. "I will also send a footman ahead with a note to my sister. She would enjoy the role of companion for a short time."

After sanding the letter, folding it, and sealing it, he pulled the cord again.

The butler appeared instantly, as if he had been waiting beyond the door for the call. James met him at the door, handed him the letter, and spoke so quietly, Izzy couldn't make out what was said.

Turning back to her, James looked at her fondly. "I have enjoyed having you stay with me, Elizabeth, and I will miss you when you leave, but I do think it is for the best." He let out a chuckle. "I have feared exposure for too long and my nerves need a rest."

"Don't worry, no one will find out. Anyway, I'll probably be gone before I see you or anyone again."

"I can see your sadness. However, I am certain you will find a man of good standing in time."

Izzy took a sip of tea. *In time*. She had already found a man of good standing in time—in 1812, to be precise.

ONCE SHE WAS SETTLED IN THE COACH, IZZY GAZED AT THE massive Chodstone Hall and said a silent goodbye.

Not wanting to see Edward again before she left, she was glad when James told her he was still at Wellsneath. She wasn't surprised to learn Alice had taken Vera there as well, but her heart ached at the thought of Vera and Edward together. Tears stung her eyes and she blinked them back. She wasn't going to cry. Lucy sat across from Izzy and thankfully kept quiet.

It was silly anyway. Edward and Vera belonged together.

Pain filled her chest. It was like someone had removed her life organ and what remained was utter emptiness. She snorted at the stupid metaphor. Although she knew she was being ridiculous, that didn't stop the tears, and with handkerchief in hand, she sobbed like a baby.

CHAPTER 17

Edward greeted his mother and Vera in the back parlor. He frowned at his mother. "Did Miss Davis not accompany you?"

"No, she is busy writing and if you were about to ask after the duke, he has work to do himself."

He eyed Vera, then faced his mother. "Have you come home to stay or are you just visiting?"

A look of impatience swept over Lady Wellsneath's face. "We are going back to Chodstone Hall, if that's what you want to know." She smiled then. "Vera wanted to see your vineyards so do be a good host and show them to her."

The room seemed to darken as if the sun had hidden behind a cloud at her revelation, and a feeling of unknown gloom ran down Edward's backbone. Why? Had he been so besotted with Elizabeth that her very absence from a room sent him into a decline?

He bowed and backed out of the door. "I have some urgent accounts to look into first." As he exited, he said over his shoulder, "I'll have tea brought to you in the meantime."

Once seated behind his desk, he and his steward began

work. The feeling of gloom spread and deepened, and he had a sense of impending doom. He rubbed his face with his palms. He wasn't usually so dramatic, but something had him all a-dither and he could not concentrate on the books.

For some inexplicable reason, Edward pushed the pile of books to his steward and left the manor. He rode posthaste back to Chodstone Hall.

He didn't know why his stomach roiled but something was wrong. He knew it in his gut. And that something urged him on in great haste.

Rounding the drive, he pulled Jupiter up and slid off the horse's back. The butler opened the door before he could knock. "My lord?"

"I am here to see Miss Davis."

"Miss Davis has departed the Hall and taken the carriage to London. Did you want to speak to His Grace?"

"When did she leave?"

"At least twenty minutes ago."

Without so much as another word, Edward leapt down the stairs, mounted his horse, and left Chodstone Hall.

EDWARD PUSHED HIS HORSE FAST DOWN THE ROAD THAT LED to London town. He looked to his side and saw a coach far ahead driving along the winding road as it trailed down the valley. A phaeton, travelling in the direction of Chodstone Hall, slid around a bend ahead of the coach. The fool driving the phaeton nearly rolled the thing. However, even after such a close call, the driver kept urging his horses forward. The coach moved to the far side of the road to give the vehicle room to pass safely. The phaeton sped past the already frightened horses and they bolted.

The coach driver's distraught shouts floated up on the

wind and, although Edward wanted to give the phaeton driver a piece of his mind, he urged Jupiter into a gallop and raced after the out-of-control coach.

Fear made the coach horses headstrong and unruly. The coach swayed dangerously. Jupiter gained on them. *Not swiftly enough*. They were rapidly coming up to a turn in the road and if he didn't catch them, they would end up in the river.

Edward leaned over Jupiter's neck. As if sensing his master's urgency, the horse stretched his neck forward, lengthened his stride, and increased his pace.

The turn was less than a mile ahead. Edward shouted. "Go, Jupiter, go."

As they came alongside the coach, a bonneted head appeared at the window. Elizabeth? Her eyes, wild with fright, sent Edward's heart into his throat.

She ducked her head out. "Edward!"

His heart fluttered in his chest at her plea.

He careered past. "Stop them," he shouted to the driver.

"I can't."

"Blast it all." A younger Edward wouldn't have been worried about breaking his neck, but somehow age had discouraged meaningless heroics. However, he had to stop those bloody horses.

He let Jupiter keep pace with the closest horse's head, held his breath, and jumped the gap. His foot caught under him as he landed on the panic-stricken horse, and he fell across the animal's back.

Grabbing the harness to stop sliding completely over the horse's side, he scrambled up and managed to maneuver his legs to sit astride. Keeping hold of his mount with one hand, he leaned to the side and grabbed the other horse's bridle just below the ear with his other. He yanked back on both bridles with as much force as he could muster. "Heave," he shouted to the driver.

Both put in their best efforts. The coach hit a rut. The driver let out a loud oath. Edward glanced behind and the coach jerked from side to side with so much force that Elizabeth was flung out of the door.

Her maid screamed.

Edward swore. He couldn't jump off the horse now. He had to stop the coach before it careened into the river—the river that was only yards away.

Between his and the driver's mighty exertions, the horses finally slowed and then stopped.

Edward leapt off his mount and raced back to Elizabeth, who was lying still on the road. He yelled over his shoulder at the coach driver. "Keep them in hand, man."

Falling to his knees, Edward threaded his hands under Elizabeth's shoulders and scooped her up so that her head rested against his chest. She was pallid and motionless. *Please don't be dead.* He gazed down into her pale face. "Please, Elizabeth, I beg of you, open your beautiful eyes."

Her eyes fluttered and her still-pink lips opened. "You saved us."

Edward caught her into him more tightly. "You live," he breathed out on a relieved sigh.

She pushed away and her hand immediately cradled her head. "Ooh, that hurts."

"Be still. Do you think you have broken any bones?"

She thought for a moment, then shook her head. "No. I think I'm in one piece."

"Good." He helped her to stand. She groaned and rubbed her back, but she appeared well. "Where were you going at this late hour?"

She turned her head in the direction she had come. "I'm going back to London. I have wor...things to do there before I leave England."

Fighting to breathe through his tightening chest, Edward

glared at her. "You are cutting your stay at Chodstone Hall short so you can—what were you going to say before you changed your mind? Work?"

Her eyes flickered and she caught her bottom lip in her teeth. "Yes, it is a kind of work. I want to finish writing my book before I...ah... sail." She gave him an open smile.

A frown brought his brows together. Sometimes she looked so proud of herself for saying a simple word. This time it was *sail.* His frown deepened. It was not a difficult word to say even for a small child.

CHAPTER 18

Izzy couldn't take her eyes off Edward as he checked the horses. He seemed to have an affinity with them. The bay mare tossed her head in the air at his approach but as he whispered something in her ear, the horse visibly relaxed. Izzy realized, as it was with her little mare at home, the animal needed to have confidence in her handlers and Edward was showing the horse she could trust him. Izzy's heart flipped at the care he showed the animals, and she warmed to him even more.

She bit her lip. Should she stay? How could she say no? He had just saved her life. Everything the man did had her caring for him a little more. She bent her head. She couldn't risk hurting him or his family by intruding on their lives, the lives that were already history to her. But every part of her screamed to get closer to him.

No man had ever had her so infatuated, no man had spurred the desire that overcame her body at his nearness, no man had ever made her want to give up her virginity so desperately, and she couldn't give a hoot if it was before marriage or even in lieu of marriage.

She clasped her hands and stuck her fingernails into the flesh of her opposing hand to stop herself thinking about that last thought. Not even the pain provoked by her nails could stop her from thinking that she would forever grieve leaving the man now walking toward her.

He stopped and took her hand, bowing. He never took his near-black eyes off her as he gently turned her hand over and kissed the hammering pulse on her wrist. Even through the thickness of her travelling gloves, she could feel his hot breath. And she was certain he could feel and hear her throbbing pulse, not only in her wrist but vibrating through her chest.

As if answering her thoughts, his eyes darkened even more.

He pressed his lips harder against her hand then stood up. "I would be honored to escort you back to Chodstone Hall," he said in a throaty voice.

All thought of going to London flew from her mind. "Thank you." She was surprised her voice sounded as husky as it did. She didn't do husky.

He helped her back into the carriage, spreading his hand low on her back. Her skin burned at his touch, but it was slow and sensuous rather than painful. She hurried to sit before her legs gave out under her. Where did the thought of a sensuous burn come from? She had never in her life thought the things she was thinking. The phrases she used must have been drawn from the very air of the early nineteenth century. The time and place must interfere with a human brain's workings.

She turned her head to the opposite window to hide the heat that rose through her body, up her neck, and fanned out through her face.

ALICE DESCENDED THE STAIRS AS THE BUTLER LED IZZY AND Edward into the front parlor.

"Ah, there you are, Edward."

"Mother."

"Yes, now don't act surprised. After you disappeared, it was natural we would return to Chodstone Hall." She looked at Izzy. "Where have you been?"

"I went for a ride," Izzy replied.

Alice frowned. "A 'ride?'"

"Yes...ah... in the carriage."

Giving a small shake of her head and smiling, Alice said, "You Americans have some strange terminology. You are just in time for tea."

"I'll just go and freshen up first."

As Izzy climbed the stairs, Alice's voice floated up. "How could you leave us like that, Edward? Vera has been pining away for you all day."

Izzy's heart sank. What was she thinking? How could she have agreed to return? Then it sank a bit further. *What will James say?*

It didn't take long for her to find out. Not two minutes after she arrived in her room the door flew open.

"Elizabeth."

His cool brown eyes bored into her, so she tried to be cute. "Oh, hi James, long time no see."

He shook his head and chuckled. "While I am slightly surprised to see you back, it is not wholly unexpected. And I must admit, I was already missing your pretty face. However, I must again warn you not to interfere in our time. It worries me greatly that your presence hasn't already meddled with history."

"Well, if it has, there's nothing we can do about it now. Actually, I was thinking my presence might have done some good. No, wait and hear me out. For one thing, you and

Edward are... maybe not chums, but definitely closer than you were before I arrived." He raised his brows at that, but to stop him from saying anything, Izzy quickly added, "And another thing—I wonder if he would be so agreeable to your marrying his mother if I weren't here."

He raised his brows and stroked his chin while gazing at her. And just as Izzy couldn't take the silence any longer, humor sprang into his eyes and he laughed.

"I am inclined to think you are right. We will have to see if your presence continues to be beneficial. Lucy will collect you for dinner."

And with that he strode from the room.

THAT NIGHT AFTER DINNER, IZZY TRIED TO KEEP HER distance from Edward, but the forces of nature were against her. Thinking he was playing whist with James, Alice, and Vera, Izzy headed for the library. Maybe some research would keep her filthy mind off Edward and his sexy looks.

She'd only just begun to search for something interesting when the door opened. She turned; Edward's form took up the entire doorway.

"It is a beautiful night. I was hoping you would consent to take a stroll in the garden with me."

"I would love to, my lord."

Oh, don't be coy, Izzy. Goodness, she wanted to kiss him there and then.

Izzy wound her arm in his. They entered the garden through the library doors, and he hurried her down the steps onto the path out of sight of the house. Izzy hoped no one had seen them. As far as James knew, she had retired for the night with a book.

Edward stopped at a garden bench away from the lights

but not so far away that they couldn't see one another. The soft light and deep shadows made the whole place more romantic than she'd ever thought possible. Izzy started to sit but Edward said, "One moment."

He took off his coat and spread it on the cold seat.

"Why, thank you, my lord." She sat down, leaving enough room for him on the coat.

He eyed the seat for a moment, then paced in front of her, his expression switching from thoughtful to irritated to decisive. At the last, he stopped and turned to face her.

He raked his hand through his dark hair, piercing her with his black eyes. "I apologize for putting you in a position that would likely cause your ruin. I have no right to ask you to be alone with me. It isn't right and if you go now, you will be safe."

"I'm not going anywhere, and it would be much easier to talk if you sat down. You're giving me a crick in the neck."

He looked at her with sympathy. "You are a stranger to England and may not be aware of society's rules of honor. Men are not to be alone with young innocents."

"So, it would be okay if I weren't an innocent?"

Surprise at her words washed over his face but he regained his dour look immediately. "No, but it is much worse for an innocent's reputation than perhaps a widow."

"Well, where I come from it's quite acceptable, so please, sit." She patted the cloak beside her.

He set his jaw in another decision. She didn't know when she had begun to read his facial expressions so easily but guessed she had learned gradually from her constant perusal of his person.

He finally sat down, and she half turned to him. "I have an apology to make also. I never meant to come between you and Vera, and you shouldn't do anything rash concerning her, because I have to go home, and you will still have your life to live here."

"You still mean to return? Mayhap to your fiancé?"

She laughed. "No, no, that was over before it began."

"I don't understand."

"You see, I thought I loved a man, and we were to be married but he decided he liked my friend more than me. It's better this way anyway; he and I wouldn't have suited."

She gave him a wide smile. It was true; she and Rodney wouldn't have suited.

"Chodstone could call me out for being here alone with you. He admires you greatly."

His thigh brushed against hers, sending shivers running up the inside of her thigh. She stiffened. He frowned. *Great, now he thinks I don't like to be touched.* To repair that notion, she twisted her body further, her leg pressing against his.

He didn't move away but held her gaze, drawing her into him. She didn't know how long she had been a prisoner to his eyes, but she blinked, and the chains were broken.

"And," she said, her voice a little too husky to her own ears, "he worries about me too much. I like him but I can't live with him forever. He has his own life and I'd just get in the way."

Edward didn't say anything, just kept looking at her with those deep, dark eyes of his that seemed to ask her if she was ready to take that leap into womanhood, that leap that before now she would have never thought remotely possible with any other man.

She had to keep talking or she would jump him, and that could be truly embarrassing if she had misconstrued his expressions in any way. "Anyway, are you not involved with Vera?"

"Involved?"

"Yes... um... aren't you spoken for? Don't you have an understanding with her that you will marry one day soon?"

He closed his eyes for a second. "I do not. My mother desperately wants a match, but neither Vera nor I have made a commitment to one another and I, for one, don't intend doing so."

"I think she may have different thoughts on that."

"She is not part of this conversation. I want to learn more about you."

"Me?" She couldn't very well tell him what he wanted to know, so she held out her hands as if to show herself off and said, "What you see is what you get."

He cocked his head to the side, raising an eyebrow at her turn of phrase. but thankfully he didn't dwell on it. "I like what I see."

Familiar heat crept into Izzy's face and he smiled that bedroom smile of his. He ran his fingers along her jawline as if testing her reaction. She stayed still, absorbing his touch that had planted her in place as if she were a seed in the ground waiting to sprout. But sprout what? Devil horns or passion to at last be a true woman? More heat made the tips of her ears burn. Passion it was.

His hand slid around the back of her neck while his other tipped her chin up, and his gaze spiraled the burning heat down her torso. He slanted his head and brought his lips down on hers. Her mouth opened to him and without thought, her arms slipped around his back, her hands splaying over his hard-muscled shoulders.

Gently, he explored her mouth and sent her reeling into a place she never wanted to leave.

He backed off just enough to whisper, "Elizabeth, you must push me away for I cannot stop. I find I am ruining you. But I cannot stop. I want you. I must have you, this night and forever. I want to make you mine and love only you until the end of time."

A question drilled through the cotton wool in her mind. *Did he just say he loves me?*

Pressing his mouth onto her already swollen lips, his tongue darted in, searching for hers. She didn't want to push him away, she wanted to get closer. She pressed against his chest. She wanted to climb inside his skin.

She had kissed a few men, but never in her life had she had the urge to do such a thing. Her fuzzy brain wondered if she should stop. He didn't hesitate. In fact, he seemed even more determined to keep kissing her.

James's warning voice flitted through her mind. *Sorry, James.* Even if she had control over her body and mind at the moment, she wouldn't want to be anywhere but in Edward's arms, tasting Edward's kisses, smelling Edward's scent.

Those thoughts surprised and excited her. Hot blood flooded her body.

Izzy had never wanted to go further than necking with any other man, but her whole body cried out to be joined with Edward in every way possible. It ached for him, and she knew only he could ease the volcanic desire in her heart.

"I love you," she whispered around his kiss.

He let out another sensual moan and pulled her more firmly into his warmth.

A cough sounded somewhere in the distance. Another floated to her ears. Edward snapped his head up, their lips separating noisily.

Izzy's sight was blurred as she looked around for what had alarmed Edward. A human form stood on the path not far away. She blinked in an effort to focus.

Edward circled Izzy's waist with his hands and, holding her weight, lifted her with him as he stood up, holding her close until she regained her balance and could stand on her own two slippered feet.

"Chodstone," Edward said, his voice full of emotion. "I mean to wed Elizabeth, so you can stop scowling."

Izzy gasped.

Vera appeared from behind James, her eyes ablaze with fury.

CHAPTER 19

E dward kept Elizabeth close. Although, it was true that he never wanted to let her go, he also wanted to breathe in her soft perfume that whirled in the air around them.

"There will be no marriage," James said, his dark glare piercing Izzy. "Come here, Elizabeth."

Izzy started forward but stopped. Scrunching her skirts in her hands, she glanced from Edward to James as if trying to make up her mind. She finally gave James a wry look. "I'm sorry, James."

He lifted his head and looked down his nose at her, letting out a growl. "Come here."

Elizabeth again looked from Edward to Chodstone, confused, uncertain and... scared? Was she frightened of the duke? What had the man done to make her fear him so?

"You have no right to command her obedience," Edward said. "She is of age and can make up her own mind."

"She is a bluestocking harlot," Vera spat.

James turned his scowling, angry face to Vera. "You will not talk about my affianced that way. Apologize to the lady."

Elizabeth expelled a noisy breath of air. "James..."

Edward felt like a knife had sliced through his heart. *It's true? She's to marry Chodstone? What of Mother? Has everyone been lying all this time? How can I have not known?*

Too many questions raced through Edward's mind, but one question stood bright. Had Elizabeth been playing with him? Snapping his head toward Elizabeth, Edward raised his eyebrow in question.

Her still-frightened eyes went wide with surprise and... was that anger? Anger at him for putting her into this position? She shook her head.

"I am sorry, James, but I refuse to apologize to that, that thing." Vera moved forward and hit Edward's arm with her fan. "Edward, your mother is sending out the banns for our marriage tomorrow. I am appalled you could do this to me, but I am willing to forget for propriety's sake."

Confusion muddled Edward's brain. What about honor? What about society's rule that ruining an innocent meant marriage? Why wasn't James demanding such? Mayhap he misunderstood their predicament.

"I am honor-bound to take this woman to be my wife and nothing either of you can say will change that."

James stepped forward and pulled Elizabeth away from Edward. "Think of your mother, Wellsneath. Have you no care as to what a scandal like this would do to her? The banns for your marriage are all but out. The *ton* know of the match. Your mother will be most upset if this was to be made public. She would be devastated if her family was scandalized." He stabbed his gaze at Elizabeth, the warning of silence apparent to Edward. "This will go no further. You will marry me and Wellsneath will marry Lady Crompton."

Vera smiled a calculating smile as she took Edward's arm in hers. "Think about your mother, darling. As James said, she would be devastated. You can't mean to hurt her."

His mother's aggrieved face whipped into his mind and he felt himself caving. He would do anything not to hurt her. He gazed at Elizabeth.

Angry color filled Elizabeth's cheeks as she stared at her guardian. "I can't marry you, you know that."

He glanced at Vera before narrowing his eyes at Elizabeth. "Edward's reputation is of paramount importance here."

Edward frowned. Why could she not marry him? Something was being said that he wasn't privy to. Elizabeth pressed her lips together tightly and her eyes flashed with fury. She glared at James as if she wanted to murder him right then even if it was in front of witnesses. She obviously had not expected Chodstone to reveal their engagement. Edward eyed Elizabeth. Or was it that she was as surprised by the announcement as he was? James and Elizabeth did indeed share secrets, and Edward meant to find out what they were.

He disengaged Vera from his arm. "I will not marry you, Vera."

She huffed. "You think not? Your mother might have something to say about that." And with that she stormed off into the house. To share her news with his mother, Edward presumed.

James turned Elizabeth toward the house. "I expect we all need a good night's sleep. Good night, Wellsneath."

Edward was left standing alone staring at the retreating backs of James and Elizabeth. She was arguing with her guardian, or was he her fiancé? Edward couldn't make out their words.

CHAPTER 20

No matter what Izzy said to James, he remained resolutely mute as he all but dragged her into the house.

Izzy tried to twist out of James's grip as they mounted the stairs. "Let me go."

"If I do, will you come with me?"

Izzy didn't answer immediately, and James narrowed his steely gray eyes at her.

"Fine," she said. "I'll go, but I'm not happy about it."

"I never expected you to be, but you know as well as I this night was a mistake."

"You know Vera is down there somewhere telling Alice about our surprise engagement."

"She will understand."

Izzy snorted. "And I suppose she will go along with your little scam?"

He chuckled. "She informed me she told you about your parents."

"Yes, she knows all about me and my parents, but she likes me, you know."

"She does like you, but she also understands you have to leave here and resume your own life in the future."

But I don't want to.

❦

ONCE SETTLED IN THE LUXURIOUS TESTER BED, IZZY LET her tears flow. What had she done? How could she have gone and fallen in love with an earl—in the nineteenth century—so far from home?

It was pointless asking how it had happened. Edward was everything she had wanted in a man. He was not only handsome and charismatic, but kind and caring. It struck her then that she had fallen in love with Edward the very night they met.

She could no longer deny the way her body responded to his touch. Never having felt anything like it before, she was consumed by him. If they had been alone for any longer, she knew she would have given herself to him, wholeheartedly, ecstatically, passionately. He was the man for her even though they were from different times. She knew with a certainty, there was no man like him, no man to make her feel the way she did at his touch, no man she would ever care about more in this time or any other time.

She sobbed into the already wet pillow. What was she to do? James would insist she return home and Edward would be honor-bound to offer for Vera.

The woman would never make him happy. She didn't like children, not even her own child. She would have preferred he be left in the schoolroom with his nanny. Izzy sniffed. That was unless she needed him to trap Edward. Edward clearly loved Michael.

Her thoughts were in disarray. They kept leaping from one subject to another without making sense of any of them.

She yawned and sniffed and groaned. Wiping her swollen, tired eyes with the sheet, she finally found peace in sleep.

❦

THE NEXT MORNING, LUCY ARRANGED IZZY'S HAIR IN A loose chignon at the nape of her neck. While the abigail worked, Izzy was wondering when James would summon her. A knock on the door answered her silent query.

Lucy answered it and after a short, hushed conversation, turned to Izzy. "His Grace would like to see you in his library."

Sighing, Izzy took one last look at her reflection in the mirror. She was pale and hollow-eyed and if she hadn't known better, she would have thought she looked like someone who was about to walk to the gallows.

She snorted as she stood up. When had her thoughts become so melodramatic? It must have been the era. Perhaps the very air she breathed.

❦

SHE WAITED FOR THE BUTLER TO ANNOUNCE HER, THEN strode into the library with her chin up and her back straight. James wasn't going to intimidate her, not if she could help it.

James put down the book he was reading on the small table beside his great wingback chair and stood up. "Ah, Elizabeth, please sit down." He indicated the damask sofa in front of the fire.

Relieved that the anger he had exuded the night before had apparently abated, Izzy took her seat.

He rounded his desk and propped a hip on the corner of the dark wood. "I understand you are young and inexperienced but, Elizabeth, you cannot become involved with someone from this time."

Izzy opened her mouth to argue.

"No, let me finish first then you can have your say. I realize I am repeating myself, but I say again, you cannot become romantically or otherwise involved with someone from this time. Especially Lord Wellsneath. His life must go on as if you had never met him." He began pacing between the settee where Izzy sat and the fire.

"Already I am worried about your mark on the man. He was all set to marry Lady Crompton and now has apparently got it into his too-honorable head that he must marry you. This is not your time. Your life must be lived in your present, not ours. Please try to understand—you will hurt him more by encouraging his feelings than if you cut him off immediately. I will miss you, for I have grown fond of you, but you must return." He smiled. "I would like it to be your decision to return. I find I have no like for sending you away."

Sitting beside Izzy, he took her hand. "Think. If you continue as you are, he will be devastated when you leave, and you must leave, Elizabeth. You must return to your own time."

Guilt flooded through Izzy at his words. He was right. She couldn't stay in that time. A memory of Edward's arms about her ran through her core. Could she live without ever knowing that feeling again? Never knowing what it was like to feel so connected to another human being? Edward was the one, and there would be no other. But even knowing she would be meddling with time and people's lives, her mind screamed, *Why can't I stay?*

She pierced James with a gaze. "Why can't I stay? My sister stayed in 1746, and as far as we know, it changed nothing."

He leapt up with a huff. "There is no way of knowing what effect she had on the world's timeline, and it does not signify. *You* cannot stay. No. If you don't agree to speak to Wellsneath, to tell him you are leaving to return to America, you give me no choice but to send for your siblings and have them retrieve you."

"You're bluffing. You can't do that."

He strode to his desk and, whisking a key from his waistcoat pocket, he unlocked and opened a drawer. "I have this and I will use it, my girl."

Izzy's eyes widened in shock at the time orb. "No," she whispered, unable to get her voice box working properly.

His voice lowered and his eyes filled with pain. "I do not want our parting to be one of rancor. As I have repeatedly said, I have a fondness for you."

Izzy cleared her throat. "If I do as you say."

He shot her a wry look.

"Hang on," Izzy said. "You told them we were engaged. Won't they think it strange that your fiancée dumped you?"

"If by dumped, you mean left me, I will think of some plausible reason for you doing so."

Tears built up behind Izzy's eyes. "Can I at least have time to think about it?"

His gaze softened as a tear slid down Izzy's cheek. "You will have the time it takes us to prepare for our journey to London. We leave in the morning and I expect you to have spoken to Wellsneath by then." He walked to the door and turned. "I will give you time to collect yourself."

"But I..." Izzy let her words trail off as the door closed behind James.

She was going to argue she hadn't finished her book, but it wasn't about the book any longer. She didn't care if she ever wrote another word, let alone an entire novel. Her heart wasn't in it any longer. Her heart had been given to Edward, every cell of the life-giving organ. And if he didn't hold it, love it, sustain it—it would die, and her body along with it.

CHAPTER 21

Edward decided to take an early morning ride
through Chodstone Hall's lush fields, hoping that
would clear his mind after a restless night of questions with no answers. But he'd only half crossed the first
field when he turned Jupiter around. "Back to the stable,
boy."

Jupiter picked up his pace. "Ah, you want your breakfast.
That is understandable, but we'll walk back, or you will be
too hot to eat."

As if the horse understood him, it relaxed and walked on
while Edward determined he would speak with Elizabeth and
demand she answer his questions.

By the time Edward had returned from his ride, his
mother had left word with the butler that she had everything
packed and was waiting for him in the front parlor.

She wrung her hands as she stood gazing into the fire, lost
in thought. Had Vera told her about the scene the night
before?

"Mother?"

She grabbed her skirts in her hands and spun on her heels. "We are leaving."

"Is this not unexpected?"

"I would think it was decidedly expected after your scene last night."

"Have you spoken to Chodstone this morning?"

"His Grace left for London before I rose, which is just as well, considering the circumstances. I have no want to speak with him at present."

Edward angled his head to peer at her drawn features. She was still a beautiful woman, who exuded all the grace a countess should, but her eyes were red and swollen. Had she been crying? He couldn't stand it when any woman cried, but his heart broke to see his mother so unhappy. He understood she would be upset over the duke's revelation that he and Elizabeth were to be married, but she seemed more upset over Edward's misdemeanor. He couldn't fathom why. Surely, she also knew he was more than willing to do the honorable thing. None of it made sense.

It wasn't as if this were the first time, he had caused a scandal. He and his friends were always getting into scrapes once they had come of age and arrived in town. He had never minded the gossip because, as he saw it, if they were talking about him and his friends, they were leaving some other poor wretch alone.

"I offered for Miss Davis."

"So I hear." She threw her hands in the air. "But what were you thinking, Edward? To seduce an innocent is one thing, but to seduce the Duke of Chodstone's ward—apparently the woman he's going to marry—is another. He could ruin you and therefore me too. He has enough power to put you in dire straits. I cannot allow it. You will not see Miss Davis or His Grace again. You will return to London with me, the banns for your wedding to Vera will be sent out, and you will retire to your country seat with your bride." She paced across the room. "You can go on with your vineyard plans and, in time, you will take your seat in the House of Lords as your father did before you and as your son will after you."

Noticing she hadn't used Chodstone's name once, he closed the distance between them and took his mother's hand to stop her from pacing. "Are you angry at me for offering for Miss Davis or are you angry at Chodstone for announcing his engagement?"

"Pshaw. I am not angry with you, I am sad for you and I am so sorry you must marry someone you do not love, but your affection for Vera will grow in time. Miss Davis cannot stay here in our—ah... England. I cannot take any more upsets. I cannot abide being the talk of the *ton*. I cannot do it anymore. You must do what is right. For you, for Vera, and for me."

But Edward didn't move; he studied his mother. There was something she wasn't saying.

A knock sounded at the door. "Come in," the countess said.

The butler pulled the door open and said, "The coach is ready, my lady."

"Thank you, Sanderson. We're coming now." She gave a pointed look at Edward and flounced out of the parlor.

Left standing there, Edward frowned. What in damnation was wrong with her? He had never seen her like this before. She was usually the essence of decorum. Her emotions were not usually so obviously displayed.

Edward followed but stopped in the foyer and asked the butler, "Where is Miss Davis?"

"She left with His Grace for London this morning, my lord."

"Did she?"

As he knew it was a rhetorical question, the butler bowed but said nothing.

With that, Edward took himself out to the coach.

※

After travelling an hour in silence, Edward could not take it anymore. "Mother, I will not marry Lady Crompton."

His mother narrowed her eyes at him. "I will hear no more about it. The banns are already sent."

"I care not about the banns. I will not be subjected to a marriage without affection."

"A good marriage rarely begins with affection. You have always understood that."

She had him there. He had thought he had no choice but to agree to the arranged marriage. But that was before Elizabeth. Before he knew what it was like to feel something for a woman, to feel something other than lust. Not that he didn't lust after the beautiful American, but he also liked her. He started. He did like her. She was funny, kind, and cared for others before her own wants. The day at the fete proved that. She had so wanted the last purple ribbon at the stall. However, when a small child became upset that she had bought it, she asked why. Once she found out the child wanted it for her mother's birthday, Elizabeth gave the ribbon to her.

He gave a silent shake of his head. He knew if he couldn't have Elizabeth, there was no chance of a love match, but he still could hope for some smidgeon of affection, couldn't he?

"Mother, I know I would be a fool to expect a love match, but I want to choose my own bride. I will not marry a woman whose only want is a title and wealth."

"You will become fond of her with time. My father

arranged my marriage, as did your father's father, and we got on fine."

"Really? What about father's mistresses? Are you telling me you were happy to be married to such a man?"

Alice flinched and, with tears glistening in her eyes, pointedly stared out of the window.

Edward mirrored her flinch. Charming. How could he be so cruel to his own mother, the woman who tried desperately to keep him from coming to his father's attention when his father was deep in his cups? And when his father did seek him out for some imagined wrong or other, the woman who took time to rebuild his self-esteem, the woman who would tell him repeatedly he was worth so much more, he could do anything he put his mind to, nothing was out of his reach if he were an honorable man, an honest man, a sympathetic man?

All the things his father was not.

His father, Edward Cavendish, the late Earl of Wellsneath, had brought up his son and namesake in his shadow. When he was young, Edward would do anything to make his father proud. But when his father took him to a club, a club no honorable man on the *ton* would enter, the earl had said that the Prince Regent attended the parties at such clubs and that made it respectable, at least in the *ton*'s eyes.

Edward, however, had no stomach for such things, and refused to go again. It was at that time that his relationship with his father became strained, and his father began to demean Edward at every opportunity, especially when deep in his cups.

He glanced at his mother's profile. Her sad eyes stared unfocused over the gentle swells of land full of grazing sheep and cattle.

He wanted to apologize, to take back what he had said, but in truth he could do no such thing. His father, her husband, was all those things and more. Edward determined to find a way to make it up to her, to have her smile again once they arrived in London.

However, once they regained the Wellsneath townhouse, his mother sequestered herself away in her rooms claiming a headache and asking not to be disturbed.

Unable to speak to his mother and restless after the long coach ride, on that first day in London Edward found himself in front of Chodstone House.

He rushed up to the door and knocked before he could change his mind. He had to speak with Elizabeth whether Chodstone liked it or not.

A footman not known to Edward opened the door. "My lord?"

"I'm here to see Miss Davis."

"Are you Lord Wellsneath?"

"Yes, what of it?"

The footman shut the door and a few seconds later, he opened it and handed Edward a letter. Before Edward could say anything, the footman shut the door once more.

Scrunching the letter in his fist, Edward strode home. Once he was in the library and seated behind his desk, he smoothed out the letter, broke the seal, and read it.

Dear, dear Edward,

I'm sorry but I cannot see you again. We are not suited.

Goodbye.

Yours truly,

Elizabeth (Izzy)

Edward reread the letter, trying to find something there that would answer his questions, but all it did was raise more. He grunted and threw the letter down. *Women are untrustworthy creatures.*

Two days passed and still Alice wouldn't see him. That put Edward out of sorts, and he spent most of his time at White's, trying to get Elizabeth out of his thoughts and ruminating on his mother's behavior. White's suited his mood with its dark, somber atmosphere and old clientele.

Even when his father's adulterous ways were the talk of the *ton*, he had never seen his mother so sad. Even then, she still attended the balls and soirées, holding her head high and partaking in the entertainments with her true friends, but avoiding any of the *ton*'s gossips.

During the hours he spent at the club, his mind circled from his mother to Elizabeth and back again, never coming to any real conclusions on either. But by the end of the second day, Chodstone had infiltrated his thoughts also.

Something niggled the back of his mind.

He wanted to despise Chodstone but, in all honesty, he couldn't. Something had changed during his time on tour with James and while guesting at Chodstone Hall. It was easy to dislike someone one hardly knew, but once he'd come to know Chodstone, saw how he treated his staff and friends, Edward couldn't bring himself to hate the man as his father had.

He also began wondering if all his father had told him was in truth.

The duke hadn't seemed like some rakehell and neither did his character appear unprincipled, as Edward was made to believe. However, while Chodstone hadn't seemed dishonest on the whole, something wasn't quite right about him.

Although Edward's reason told him it was unlikely, he had the strangest notion that the three people who had held his thoughts hostage these last two days were concealing some truth from him.

Resolved to find the truth of the matter, he left White's in the late afternoon and made his way home.

Upon entering the townhouse, he was delighted to see Larson carrying a tea tray across the foyer to the front drawing room. "Larson, is Lady Wellsneath in there?"

Larson stopped, setting the teacups jingling. "Yes, my lord."

Entering the room after the butler, Edward was stunned to find Lady Vera Crompton visiting. He hadn't seen her before they left Chodstone Hall and, in truth, he had hoped never to see her again.

"Ah, Edward," his mother said, standing with a flourish. "I was just telling Vera, I have a previous appointment. Please do accommodate her while I am gone."

Edward placed his hat on a seat and narrowed his eyes at her smiling face. Her eyes were bright, a sign of happiness, and her smile was genuine. What had happened to so change her disposition?

Carriage wheels sounded directly outside the townhouse. Alice glanced out of the window and immediately swept from the room, calling for her pelisse and parasol the moment she entered the foyer.

Going to the window, Edward was stunned to see Chodstone's crest on the now stopped carriage. With the top open, Chodstone's profile was easily recognizable as the duke held the reins of two of the finest horses Edward had seen. The bays, perfectly matched, must have cost some blunt at Tattersall's.

What was his mother doing going about with the duke, a man affianced to another?

Vera's cloying lavender scent swirled through the air, reminding him of his unwelcome guest. He turned to find her close, snaking her hand toward his arm. Aware she was about to link her arm in his, he stepped out of her reach.

Her hand hung there for a moment before she waved it around as if that had been her intent all along.

"I'm so glad you are here, darling. Have you seen the paper today? The banns are out and the date is set."

"The date for what?"

"Our wedding, of course."

He huffed. What was his mother thinking? He refused to be shackled to the woman. "I will retract the notice immediately."

"You can't do that. I will be the talk of the *ton*. No. I will not allow you to ruin my... my son's life."

"Don't bring Michael into this. His life will not be ruined if you have the grace to stop encouraging my mother in her endeavors to marry me off. I am not on the marriage market now, nor will I be in the future. There will be no scandal. Coin will have them printing a retraction, citing the paper's mistake."

"You are not the same man you were just a few weeks ago, my lord. I fear Miss Davis has fogged your mind. I understand you are physically attracted to her, as is James, but you cannot think for a moment she would make an ideal countess. She has no brains for dealing with servants or running the manor of an earl."

"But she will make an ideal duchess?"

"I doubt James will go through with the marriage once he takes what he wants, and from what I have heard, they are already privately acquainted."

Although Edward knew she was lying, his gut convulsed at the thought of Chodstone, of anyone, touching Elizabeth. She was his.

He rubbed his chin. Could she still be his? He still suspected her of secrets, but even so, he didn't care. He wanted only her in his life, now and always. Whatever kept her from dealing with him, he would overcome.

Edward turned his cold eyes on Vera. "I have no like for gossip."

All Edward wanted at that moment was to be out of Vera's presence and to talk to Elizabeth. But how? His mother had arranged his marriage. And he couldn't fault her for posting the banns because, before Elizabeth, he had been content enough with the idea.

He had promised his brother he would look after Vera and their son, and Edward was extremely fond of Michael. He was also in need of an heir and a countess for his estates so he could spend more time building up his investments.

He frowned. It had seemed the most satisfactory arrangement at the time.

However, that was all before Elizabeth crashed—he hid a smile—into his life. He had to think this through, but first he had to withdraw the marriage notice without scandal.

He bowed low, hoping the threat in his eyes would silence Vera. "I bid you farewell, my lady." He strode to the door and angled his head back.

"Have the phaeton readied," he commanded Larson, who was pretending to arrange a vase of flowers on the table near the drawing room door.

CHAPTER 22

Glad to be back in London, Izzy sat working, or at least trying to work, at her small table in her room at Chodstone House. The room was smaller than her chambers at Chodstone Hall, but it was cozy and comfortable.

After staring at the blank sheet of paper for who knew how long, Izzy wiped the now dried pen nib as best she could and stood up. Maybe a walk in the garden would clear her head.

She stood at the wardrobe, staring at the clothes without seeing.

Edward wouldn't stay out of her thoughts. Touching her fingers to her mouth, she could feel his lips, taste that kiss. Tears sprang into her eyes at the thought of never seeing him again, let alone touching him.

She let out a long, noisy breath and snatched up the first spencer in her reach.

It wasn't as if his sexy form were the only thing she liked about the man. He was everything she had unconsciously wished for in a man. She widened her eyes in surprise. Everything she wanted in a husband. She rubbed her eyes. How would she ever find someone like him again?

Someone who cared about his family, someone who loved children, someone who was kind to those in his employ. She snorted and glared at her reflection in the wall mirror. "Someone who is engaged to be married to someone else."

With the spencer in hand, she plopped onto the bed. "What should I do?"

She thought about her own time. She loved and missed her family and her own room in the family house. She fit in there, at least to the outside viewer. She was a respected writer and her own boss, but somehow that was never enough to make her feel she truly fit in. She always felt out of step, no matter how busy she kept—and she was always busy. There was always something she could do, whether it was writing, organizing her schedule, lunching or dining with agents, publishers, directors, script writers. She huffed. But had she been happy? If she was honest—and she always tried to be, at least with herself—she wasn't. She was always trying to find that safe place, the place where she fit.

In 1812, though, she drew comfort from the rules of society. She liked them, and even though she wasn't busy every moment of the day, she didn't care. A walk in the garden filled her with satisfaction like no seven-figure contract ever could. She enjoyed the manners of the time, the courtesy, and especially the chivalry. Edward had saved her life, for gosh sake. She couldn't think of one man who would risk his neck for her in modern times.

Laying the spencer over her lap, she absently picked at a small loose thread. But she definitely didn't fit outwardly in Edward's time. If there were to be any chance, she could stay where she was, she would have to learn how to go on. She smiled at that turn of phrase in her thoughts. Even now, she was beginning to think in the way people of this era spoke.

She snorted and immediately berated herself for the unladylike noise.

"Maybe... no—mayhap—I can stay."

The words appeased her soul. She laughed. Cheerful once again, she pulled on the spencer as she stood up. And there was a spring in her step as she made for the door. She paused. Edward's marriage notice in the paper that morning popped back into her mind.

Well, he wasn't the only reason she wanted to stay. He was a big reason, a major reason, an enormous reason, but not the only reason. The time suited her perfectly even if she couldn't have Edward. Oh, but to have him would be so sublime.

Vera Crompton's sour image appeared in her mind. How he could agree to live a lifetime with that cow, she didn't know. She shuddered. But then Michael's smiling face replaced Vera's. Of course, Edward felt responsible for his friend's son. Izzy knew he loved the boy, and Michael was the sweetest little thing she had known, so she understood why.

As her hand touched the door handle, a knock sounded on the other side. She opened it and stared at the silver tray the butler was holding.

"You have a caller, Miss Davis."

She questioned him with a look, expecting him to tell her who.

He angled his head and gave a slight nod to the tray.

Izzy followed his eyes. The only thing on the tray was a small folded card.

She snapped the card up. "Couldn't you just tell me who it is?"

Unfolding the card, Izzy noted his lips twitch in a hidden smile and she wondered just how much Hampton knew. He never seemed perturbed at her lack of regal manners. In fact, the lack of them seemed to amuse him. She wondered then what the other servants thought of her, but her thoughts stopped there. The card was Lady Vera Crompton's calling card. Izzy had to stop herself from rolling her eyes. It was as if her thinking about the woman had somehow summoned her.

Plonking the card back on the tray, she said, "Thank you, Hampton. Where did you put her?"

"Lady Crompton is in the front parlor, miss. Would you like tea served?"

Rum and coke, please. But she nodded. "Yes, thank you."

With that, she swept by the butler and made her way down the stairs. Pausing outside the parlor, she took a breath and let it out slowly. *Keep calm, keep calm.*

Vera, seated on the blue settee, looked to all the world like a princess with her pink day dress and straight back, although to Izzy's eyes, the small puffy sleeves only accentuated the width of her shoulders. The sneer on the woman's upper lip suggested Lady Crompton thought herself in some stench-filled sewer pit instead of Chodstone's lovely blue parlor scented by freshly cut roses and lavender.

"Lady Crompton." Izzy made her appearance with a small bob of a curtsy. She wasn't going to go all out for the woman, especially when Vera had that you're-so-less-than-me look on her face.

She didn't even bother to stand but instead honored Izzy with the slightest bow of her head. "Miss Davis." She smiled but only with her mouth. "How good to see you."

Taking the chair near the low table, Izzy said, "And you."

"It is such a lovely day out today I was wont to take a walk, and I thought, how nice to visit Miss Davis and His Grace."

"I'm afraid His Grace is out at present."

She waved her hand. "No matter. Have you received an invitation to the Marchioness of Brampton's soirée tonight?"

"Yes, I believe we did."

"Divine. The *on-dit* has it that the marchioness's daughter has a beautiful voice for singing opera. I am so looking forward to hearing her."

"I am too." Izzy stopped a frown from lining her forehead and kept her expression as pleasant as possible. The woman was up to something, but she couldn't for the life of her think what. She couldn't fault her manners, and Vera did seem truly excited by the prospect of the soirée, but something in her eye had Izzy fidgeting with her skirt.

She clasped her hands in her lap.

Vera smiled a cat-who-caught-a-mouse smile. "Have you seen the papers this morning?"

"Yes." Izzy had a hunch her real reason for visiting was about to be revealed.

"I knew the banns were to be posted today but I had no idea the date for the marriage would be so soon. I am beside myself with excitement that Edward went out of his way to obtain a special license."

Izzy blanched. A special license? Was he so angry that James had announced she was engaged to him that he would hurtle headlong into a loveless marriage? She hadn't had the chance to speak to him after that night but now she decided she must, and soon.

Vera wasn't finished with her, though. "You don't believe Edward would be honorable to someone as inconsequential as you, do you? That little escapade in the garden at Chodstone Hall was his way of saying goodbye to his roguish ways. Of course, he might have seen you as a possible mistress, but I have put my foot down about that. I will not put up with my husband taking mistresses like the rest of the gentry, and he has promised not to do so."

The butler knocked and pushed the slightly open door out of his way so he could keep both hands on the tea tray.

Vera stood up and wandered to the window as the tray was placed on the table.

Izzy tried to pull up a smile. "Thank you, Hampton."

He bowed, but Izzy noted the look of concern in his eyes, so she widened her smile before he turned and left.

As if she was just waiting for the sound of the door to close, Vera spun around, her soft-pink muslin floating in the breeze. "You cannot have thought Edward would be interested in you for more than a brief dalliance."

Heat filled Izzy's cheeks. "How dare you?"

"You are not suitable to be a countess. Although the *ton* may never hear of it, you are ruined in Edward's eyes. He would never lower himself to a match with someone so free with their favors." She spun on her heels and gazed out of the window. "And to think, you were already affianced to the duke." She turned back. "I think you will make a poor duchess, but that is the duke's decision, not mine."

Izzy stood up, clenching her hands into fists at her sides so hard that her nails bit into the soft flesh of her palms.

Vera swept past Izzy to the door and turned back. "I find I have no liking for tea at this time of day. Good day, Miss Davis."

The woman's walking shoes clicked over the tiles of the foyer. Hampton must have been waiting at the door, because there was no stutter in her steps as she clicked down the stairs.

Izzy plonked back down into her chair then leapt back up and started pacing the parlor. Grief ripped through her and she gasped at the strength of the hurt in her heart. She had thought she could live there without Edward. She had thought she could handle him marrying another. But she now knew in her heart, she would be pained to the core every time she saw him with his wife. There was no way her heart could handle watching Edward marry Vera. And to protect herself, she would have to leave. As soon as James returned, she would tell him she had to go home.

As she exited the parlor, Hampton held out another silver tray with a letter on it. Izzy broke the seal and read it. James would be out all day and wasn't sure when he'd return.

Izzy kept herself busy waiting for James to return and was happy to finally get close to the end of her novel, but every minute he was away, it was a minute closer to Edward's wedding the next day.

By late that evening, Izzy was yawning but tried to stay awake. She needed to leave, and she needed the orb to go. James had the thing locked away. Oh, she understood it was so no one accidentally played with it, but that didn't make her feel any better at that moment. The darn man always carried his keys with him as well, so she couldn't even use her ability to sneak and snoop to get the orb.

She had almost drifted to sleep when the sound of carriage wheels crunching on the gravel drive sounded outside. *James.* She sighed. She would speak to him first thing in the morning.

The next morning, Izzy rushed out of her room and hurried down the stairs at the same time James entered the foyer. He smiled widely at her, so widely that little lines crinkled around his eyes. She had never seen him so happy and she couldn't help but smile back.

He strode to her. "Let us talk."

He paused just long enough for her to enter the parlor.

"Please sit," he said, and once she sat on the settee, he took the wingback chair to her right.

Wondering why he looked so pleased with himself, Izzy

straightened her dress over her knees. She gazed at him, waiting.

"I've grown fond of you and I dislike seeing you so sad, so I have spent yesterday thinking about what you said about your sister and how she stayed in the past." He smiled. "And I had luncheon with Alice."

"Alice?"

"She, too, is fond of you and has concluded she should not have interfered with Edward's happiness. However, she can't retract the banns and now they are in place. The *haut-monde* and the Prince Regent will expect a wedding to take place this day."

"I know, that's why I've decided to go home."

"Home?" James raised his brows in surprise. "That's why I wanted to speak to you. After much thought, I would like you to stay."

Izzy opened her mouth to tell him she couldn't, but he held his hand up.

"During my time at Brooks'—"

Izzy couldn't help interrupting; she hadn't heard of the place. "Brooks'?"

"A club."

"Oh, I thought you'd go to White's." Nearly every gentleman in the books she read went to White's.

"Too many Tories spend their time at White's. Anyway, while I was playing faro with a friend it occurred to me that although you have developed a tendre for Wellsneath, he is by no means the only gentleman of my acquaintance. In fact, my friend, the Viscount Grisham, is a most satisfactory gentleman."

Tears burned the back of her eyes. "Oh, James, that is so sweet, and if you'd said any of that at Chodstone Hall, everything would have been different, but I can't now. The man I love is about to be married and I can't stay and see him with another."

She stood up and walked to the window. The sky was gloomy with gray clouds meandering over the bleak sky and hiding any sign of the sun. *Perfect.* She spun back to James, who had also risen and stood watching her. "Please give me the orb. I have to go home."

The spark went out of James's eyes. "I am disappointed, but I understand."

CHAPTER 23

Edward rose early and, grabbing the paper from the small table in the foyer, quickly opened it and found the retraction of the marriage banns his mother had placed. The corners of his lips turned up. It had been surprisingly easy to procure the journalist's cooperation. Of course, Edward's title helped there. The small man had gushed so much about what an honor it was to have the Earl of Wellsneath in his offices.

However, the little man wasn't so bacon-brained not to use Edward's visit to his own end. He had said he hoped no such error would affect his daughter's chances of a good match this season. The way he spoke about his daughter, he was raising some kind of breeze.

Finally, the dolt made his point clear. "Banns have been issued by mistake before, my lord, just as invitations are known to go astray from time to time. For instance, neither my wife nor myself have received the invitation to the Wellsneath Ball." He had winked then. "The *on-dit* has it, it is the ball of the season and if one held an invitation, one would be made."

He had Edward brought to Point Non Plus and Edward hadn't minded at all. "Of course. I am sure it is just an oversight, and you will have your invitation by tomorrow. In fact, if you make my introduction to your daughter, I will be sure to ask her to dance."

The cuffin had grinned widely. "The retraction will be printed in the morning edition, my lord."

Edward refolded the paper messily and, putting his hat on his head, left the townhouse.

He continued on his way, not paying attention to his surroundings and thinking all the while about Elizabeth. Did she have feelings for him as he had for her? If her reaction to his kiss meant anything, then surely, she did at least like him.

A carriage passed close by him, spraying putrid water over his Hessians. He looked up with a start but before he could voice his complaint, he stopped and stared at the long drive before him.

His feet had taken him along a well-known route but instead of steering him toward the park, they brought him to Chodstone House. His subconscious knew all too well that was where Elizabeth resided and it also knew if he didn't ask, he would never discover her true feelings.

With a deep intake of breath, he made his way up the drive to knock on the shiny black doors.

Hampton opened the door and gave Edward a bow of his head. "My lord?"

"Is Miss Davis in?"

"Who is asking?" Chodstone's voice came from behind Hampton, who pulled back to reveal Edward.

"Ah well, come in, young man. I don't like talking on the house step."

Hampton opened the door further and once Edward stepped over the threshold, he quietly closed it again.

"This way." Chodstone climbed the stairs to the first landing without waiting to see if Edward followed him.

Edward did and once in the study, he sat in the chair the duke indicated.

"I presume you are looking for Miss Davis?"

"Yes."

"I'm afraid she is no longer here."

"Where is she?"

"She has gone home."

Edward pressed his lips together. She was gone? Did she not care for him in the least? How could she go without speaking so much as a word to him?

He swallowed, trying to digest the duke's information, finally blurting out, "I am sorry for your loss."

Chodstone nodded. "I will indeed miss her."

"I would have expected you to be more upset."

"I always knew she would leave. I just hope we may meet again in the future."

The small smile playing on Chodstone's lips befogged Edward's mind. "Are you not upset to be so cast off?"

"Cast off? What are you talking about, man?"

"Your broken engagement."

"Engagement?" Chodstone eyed him warily as if he'd forgotten he'd made the revelation openly, but then a smile formed on his lips. "Ho, you think me engaged to Miss Davis? No, many times no. I am bereaved to say I lied. I said that to save Miss Davis embarrassment and to get her away from you, and I couldn't have Lady Crompton spreading gossip about my ward."

He swooped some papers up off the desk and tapped them into a pile.

Edward regarded the duke. "Lady Crompton has not kept your disclosure of your impending marriage to Miss Davis a secret."

"I suppose I should have thought of that. Never mind, with Miss Davis gone our engagement can be broken after a time without any scandal. And with the talk of impending war with America, our broken engagement will be of no consequence. But there is you. You are to be married today."

Edward shook his head. "No, there is a retraction of the banns in this morning's paper, stating the paper was at fault."

The duke eyed Edward. "That is interesting news, interesting indeed."

Chodstone went back to his papers and Edward stood, knowing when he was being dismissed.

Making his way back to his townhouse, his steps were heavy. So too was his heart. Would he ever see Elizabeth again? Mayhap, he could venture to America. He had to talk to her. He had to find out once and for all if he was truly a fool for thinking she had feelings for him as he had for her.

He cursed himself for not asking how she had travelled to the docks. He spun back toward Chodstone House, thinking he may yet see her before she set sail.

A carriage halted on his side of the road a horse length ahead and, as he passed by, the door opened. Vera leaned out. "Edward."

He groaned, but stopped. There were too many people about at that time of day, and to cause a scene would be the *haut ton*'s next *on-dit*.

"I was on my way to my modiste. How fortunate to see you though."

Fortunate wasn't the word that immediately came to his mind. He kept silently wishing she would say what she meant to say, and begone.

"Lady Wellsneath was caught up with planning the Wellsneath Ball yesterday, and I must say, it is going to surpass any other ball of the season."

He nodded. It always did.

"Are you unwell? Why don't you say something?"

"I am sorry, but I did not hear a question."

"Oh, Edward, you don't need to be asked a question to indulge in a conversation. Anyway, as I was saying, the ball is going to be grand. Lady Wellsneath told me Miss Davis has left London this morning and is now on her way to America. The poor duke must be devastated, but he will still be at the ball." She paused as if to read his reaction to her news. "Well, anyway, with her not here, surely you will forego the retraction of our banns and meet me at St Peter's this morning."

He smiled then. "I have already arranged the retraction. It was in this morning's early edition."

Even if he couldn't have Elizabeth, he had no intention of being shackled to Vera.

Her face reddened, and her eyes flashed in anger as she opened her mouth, but she must have thought better of making a scene right in the middle of the street because she laughed a shaky laugh and flicked her fan at him. "Don't be a ninny." Lowering her voice to a whisper, she hissed, "Your mother will demand you reinstate the banns for a different day. We are suited, Edward. Everyone knows it."

"I do not know it." He tipped his hat and head to her. "Good day, Lady Crompton."

With that, he turned from the carriage and strode back toward Chodstone House. If Elizabeth had only left this morning, she might still be at the port waiting to board, or the ship might still be docked. If so, he would find her.

CHAPTER 24

Gazing at the orb, Izzy stared at the leaf filigree. All she had to do was turn the top to align the leaves. She glanced at the mirror and frowned. Her reflection taunted her with its sad blue eyes. Stay, it seemed to say. Please, stay.

Shaking her head, she spun away and let the tears fall. She couldn't stay. She could never live there knowing Edward was married to another, no matter how much she loved this time period, no matter how much she fit in with the society of the day. She would never be a fit for Edward; she could never be a countess. Vera was right. How could she have even thought it would be possible?

She was a nobody.

Sure, peers of the realm had married Americans before, but those women were heiresses and much-sought-after ornaments of the gentry. Edward was an earl, and with that, he had a position to uphold not only in society but in Parliament. His mother was also right. Edward was suited to Vera, who already held a high position within their society.

Edward loved Vera's son and he would be a good father, a

good and caring father. Pain stabbed Izzy in the chest so hard her hand flew over her heart. She had never given much thought to being a mother, except to wonder if she would or even could be a better parent than her own had been. Abby had been more of a mother to Izzy than their biological mother.

She sighed as memories of Abby's cuddles and kisses floated through her mind. Abby had taught Izzy to love; she had taught Izzy what being a mother was. Abby had always been there for her and her siblings... until she wasn't.

Oh, how Izzy needed Abby's cuddles now. She needed her sister's strength and advice. "Ab-by." A sob broke in her throat. "If only you were here."

Blinking at the orb as she clutched it in her hand, she wondered if she could go back to Abby's time. Max would be at home, of course, but Izzy needed her eldest sister. Only Abby would do.

She would know what it was like to love a man so deeply, so completely that the thought of bearing his children sent waves of pleasure through her being. It was like nothing Izzy had ever imagined before in her life.

Izzy swiped at her tears. She loved Edward, loved nine-teenth-century England, but she had to leave, and leave she would. She twisted the top of the orb, closed her eyes, and waited for the weird falling feeling. Nothing happened, and her eyes snapped open to stare at the time device. The leaves weren't quite aligned. She tried again to turn the top, but it wouldn't budge.

Huh?

No. She had to get home. She had to see Max and Garrett. She needed her family.

She shook the orb. Maybe Garrett or Max had done something with the black orb. Why would they mess about with it when they would have known that Izzy had used the white orb?

She whispered a prayer. "Please send me home."

Flopping on the great tester bed, Izzy regarded the device with suspicion. "Why aren't you working?"

A soft knock sounded at the door. "What?" Izzy shouted.

A clunk sounded in the hall outside. Whoever was on the other side must have dropped something.

"It's... it's Lucy, miss. I have come to hang your clothes."

Izzy blanched. Poor Lucy. It wasn't her fault the orb hadn't worked. Izzy hurried and opened the door. She tried to smile as if all were fine, but she knew her face was still streaked with tears, and her lip shook with the effort. The maid widened her eyes in concern. "Are you well, miss?"

Izzy tried a better smile. "Sorry. I'm a bit busy right now. Can you come back?"

With her arms full of beautiful clothes, Lucy bobbed a small curtsy as Izzy shut the door.

Leaning against the cool, wooden door, Izzy surveyed her room. Yes, it was her room. That's the way she had come to think of it, and she would miss her room. Its floral wallpaper, with its swirls of green leaves on the palest cream background splashed at irregular intervals with red flowers, had grown on her, and the magnificent tester bed with its ornate posts and calming, sea-green fabric—that would be hard to give up.

Her eyes found her small writing bureau and she smiled. She had become used to writing longhand, even becoming somewhat proficient in the use of the ink pen.

Maybe when she got home she could remodel her room to be exactly like this one.

She sighed. She wouldn't be going home, at least not until she could figure out why the time device wasn't working.

She pushed off the door and wandered to the window, letting her fingers slide over the back of the chair as she went.

"Everything has gone wrong, and Edward is to be married this very day."

A picture of Edward standing before the vicar rose in her mind. Vera stood beside him and turned her smug smile on Izzy.

Edward would be miserable if he married Vera. Izzy let out a laugh. Maybe she should crash the wedding. She was certain if she were to see Edward's face, she would know if there was a chance for them, or at least she would know if he was intent on marrying Vera.

The banns stated they were to be married in St Peter's. The carriage driver would know where that was. Donning her cream pelisse and scooping up her reticule, Izzy hurried down the stairs.

Once she had ordered the Chodstone carriage, she waited impatiently until it was brought around to the front, her heart pumping hot blood through her veins at the thought of what she was about to do.

CHAPTER 25

Feeling Vera's cold, hard gaze on his back, Edward hurried along the street to arrive at the driveway just in time to see Chodstone's carriage wheel whirl past him and around the next corner in great haste. Only one person was in the coach and he was certain that person was Elizabeth.

"What the devil?"

He glanced at Chodstone House and back at the disappearing carriage. Chodstone had lied... again. Elizabeth hadn't left that morning, but she was leaving that very moment. Without caring if he was making a spectacle of himself, Edward ran as fast as his legs would take him to the Wellsneath townhouse, only a block away.

Crashing through the front door, he barreled past a surprised Larson and out to the mews at the back of the townhouse.

He stopped short of the ostler. "Quick, help me saddle Jupiter."

Throwing caution to the wind, he galloped his horse over the stones and around the corner he had seen Chodstone's coach take. He pulled Jupiter up. *Fiend seize it.* He had no idea from where she was to depart. If she was on her way to Liverpool, he might catch the coach before it arrived.

Edward hauled Jupiter to a stop at a street trader's cart and tipped his hat at the man. "Have you been here long?"

"Since before dawn, my lord."

"Did you happen to see a regal coach with the duke's emblem on the door?"

"Aye."

"Which way did it go?"

"I am not certain, my lord. Would you like a basket of apples?"

"No, I don't want any apples. Tell me which way the coach went."

The fellow rubbed his hairy chin. "Well," he said slowly.

Edward threw a copper to him, surprised at the old man's agility to catch it as it went high over his head.

He pointed down the road. "That way, and around the last corner."

Edward frowned at the increasingly busy street. "Are you sure?"

"Yes, my lord. I couldn't take my eyes off the horses. Magnificent beasts for sure."

Edward shook his head. The man hadn't been sure he even saw a coach not two seconds before, but it was the only clue Edward had.

Rounding the last corner, Edward stopped his horse again. It didn't make sense. No port could be found in that direction. He pushed Jupiter forward, and upon spotting the spires of St Peter's, he let out a breath of air. *Is that her destination? She thinks she is to witness a wedding?*

He rode to the church and, sliding to the ground, called out to a small boy scraping at the dirt. "You there. Can you hold my horse?"

The boy puckered up his face and continued to forage around in dirt. Edward pulled out a gold coin and showed it to him.

Even then the boy hesitated, looking between Edward and his spot of ground. He shrugged and ran over to the horse, where Edward handed him the coin. "Yes, my lord. Thank you, my lord."

Edward leapt up the stairs of St Peter's two and three at a time. Just as he scaled the last steps, Elizabeth appeared out of the inside gloom, and he halted. She stopped also and stared at him, her beautiful blue eyes sparkling with unshed tears.

He closed the distance between them and took her in his arms and kissed her thoroughly. "I thought I would not see you again," he said between kisses.

"Nor I, you."

He had to stop himself from holding her so tightly he'd crush her bones. His head swam with glee and his body shook with relief at the sight, the touch, the scent of her. "I love you."

"Oh Edward, I love you too."

He kissed her once more then finally broke away, so he could look at her. Tears streamed down her face and she blinked and wiped them from her cheeks with shaky hands. He was so happy, he laughed and gave her a handkerchief.

She laughed also. "Thank you." Wiping her nose, she gazed at him in wonder. "You aren't married?"

"No, I could not. The banns were retracted in this morning's early paper."

"I didn't see it before I left."

He took her back into his arms and kissed her mouth and cheeks, whispering in her ear. "Will you marry me?"

She stilled for a moment, and Edward had the great fear that he had misjudged their meeting.

She pulled away and gazed at him. "Oh, Edward, I do want to, but there is something you must know."

"The duke told me he lied about your engagement."

"No, that's not it."

"Are you still enamored with the man you were to marry in America?"

"No, that's not it either. There's... um... there's something you have to know before we can even think to marry."

"Nothing you can say will change my mind. I believe I fell in love with you from the moment I helped you off the ground that night in Fleet Street. I will never feel the way I do about you for anyone else, ever. Please say you'll marry me, my love."

"I can't, not until I tell you." She turned away. "Oh, blast it. How am I going to tell you?"

He clasped her shoulder and turned her around. "Nothing can be so bad."

Izzy's knees faltered at his breath on her face. *I hope you still think that when you know the truth.*

He kissed her again, and she hung onto the back of his coat so she wouldn't collapse at his feet. His kisses muddled her brain, but a small voice kept telling her he might not love her when he found out the truth. Not wanting to think about it, she kissed him back with a passion she had never felt before and one she didn't want to lose.

He backed off a bit and spread kisses along her chin to her ear. "I love you."

His voice broke her reverie and she gasped and leapt back. "I have to tell you the truth about me."

"I care not who you are nor what you have done. I care

not if you are a criminal. I love you and that is all there is need of."

He tried to pull her in again, but she twisted out of his grip. "No, no more kissing until you know the whole story." She started down the stairs. "You need to get your mother and meet me at James's house. We'll talk then."

He caught up with her and held her arm, stopping her from going further. "But I cannot kiss you there."

"You can, and trust me, I want you to kiss me." Izzy shot him a mischievous smile but quickly frowned. "But not until after we tell you everything."

"We?"

"Yeah, well, your mother and James know all about me." She pushed her hair from her face. "You coming or what?"

He studied her with tight lips and intense eyes for a moment, trying to read her mind. She was clearly nervous, and though he was curious, her strange speech and behavior had him concerned. "I will meet you at Chodstone House, but please, Elizabeth, tell me you are not already married."

"I'm not already married."

That was all he needed to know and, as he helped her into the carriage, he picked her up and kissed her again. "Then there is nothing you can tell me that will change my mind."

The corners of Izzy's mouth dropped, and she hurriedly pecked him on the lips. "I hope not."

Izzy rushed through the doors the moment Hampton opened them. "James," she shouted. "James."

Hampton stepped forward. "His Grace is in the study, Miss Davis."

"Thanks, Hampton." Izzy ran up the stairs and into the study without knocking.

"James, I need to——"

She was brought up short by James and Alice sitting together on the settee, chatting easily with one another.

Izzy tried to look confident as she sat and waited, albeit impatiently, for Edward to arrive. She clasped and unclasped her clammy hands in her lap. He said he loved her, he said he didn't care what secret she wanted to confess. He said he'd meet her at Chodstone House directly. She wasn't sure how long directly meant, but surely it wouldn't have been over two hours.

She glanced at Alice. If the woman was worried what her son would say, she didn't appear nervous in the least. James gave Izzy the same half smile that sprang to his face the moment she had told him Edward loved her. He seemed to think the whole affair was most humorous. Or maybe—ah... *mayhap*—he thought Izzy's disclosure would affect Edward so much that he wouldn't care about James and Alice marrying.

Unable to sit any longer, Izzy stood up and strode to the front window. Peeking out through the curtains, she gazed past the drive and focused on the passing traffic. Midafternoon, there was always someone coming and going from Manchester Square. A carriage turned into the drive. Her heart leapt into her throat. It was Edward's new curricle.

She spun on her heels. "He's here."

Alice pulled a sampler with a threaded needle in it out of her big bag and started working on her embroidery. "There's nothing to be nervous about. If Edward said he loves you, he loves you, and nothing will change his mind."

Izzy clasped her hands in front of her. "I hope you're right."

Hampton stood in the doorway. "The Earl of Wellsneath, Your Grace."

"Very good, Hampton, show him in."

The butler stepped aside, and Edward swept into the room, coming to a stop before James and Alice. James stood up as Edward bowed to him and then his mother. "Your Grace, Mother."

His gaze settled on Izzy and he smiled. "Miss Elizabeth."

Izzy gave him a trembling smile back and curtsied. "My lord. Please sit. Would you like some tea?"

"Not at the moment." He sat in the brown wingback chair, and his look spanned the three of them but rested on his mother. "What is this great secret Elizabeth has told me you know?"

Alice glanced up at James and nodded for him to speak.

James cleared his throat. "Elizabeth is from the future, and your mother has agreed to marry me."

Izzy gasped. She couldn't believe James just blurted it out like that. Surely, he could have taken the time to lead up to it. Izzy frowned at a giggling Alice.

Edward sat staring at James as if trying to make sense of what he had said.

"You should see your face," Alice said to Edward. "I don't think I have seen you so flummoxed."

James threw Alice a quick smile. "Do you remember Mark and Dianne? They are Elizabeth's parents and they, too, were from the future."

Edward stood up and glared at James, then his mother, then Izzy, and back at James.

"I know." James waved his hand about. "I didn't believe it at first either, but after some time in their company, hearing of their travels to different times, seeing proof of such, I came to believe, and I trusted them more than any in my life." He glanced at Alice. "With the exception of your mother, of course. She has always had my belief and trust."

"What are you talking about? Elizabeth is from the Americas, and you are not marrying my mother."

Alice put her sewing on the arm of the settee, stabbing the needle in much harder than needed. "You have no say in that and, I must say, you are being quite rude. Elizabeth?"

Izzy started; she wasn't expecting to be called on. "Yes?"

"Tell him."

Still wringing her hands, Izzy inhaled deeply. "I am from the future. So too were my parents." She pulled at her green day dress. "These are not the clothes I usually wear. At home, I do still like pretty dresses, but they are much shorter. In fact, fashion has changed a great deal from this time period. I can draw modern fashions, if you like. I'm not as good as my brother, but I think they would suit. That is, if it would that make a difference. Or you might say I am just imaginative. I agree, I am imaginative. That is why I write fiction, but as I said, I could draw some things for you. James, have you some drawing paper and—"

"Elizabeth!" Edward shouted.

Izzy jumped. "What?" She gazed at his frowning face and glanced at Alice and James, who were both smiling encouragement at her. "I'm sorry. I was rambling, wasn't I?"

Edward drew his brows together. "You most certainly were."

"Edward," Alice said, plopping her sewing in her lap. "You must—"

"No, do not say anything, Mother." He plopped onto the sofa. "No one say anything." Resting his elbows on his knees, he dropped his face into his open palms.

Izzy looked at Alice.

She shrugged and mouthed, "Give him time."

James held out his hand to Alice. "Come, my love. I have something to show you."

Alice took his hand and stood up, gave Izzy an encouraging smile, and let James guide her from the room.

"Wait," Izzy called.

James said over his shoulder, "You can handle this, Elizabeth. If Edward refuses to believe you, the time travel device is in the top drawer of my escritoire."

CHAPTER 26

E dward tried to make sense of what he had just heard, but his mind was not co-operating. The only thing he understood at that moment was that both the duke and his mother had left the room. A smile formed on his lips at that. They had done nothing but intrude on Edward and Elizabeth for months and now suddenly, they leave them alone? He peeked through his fingers. And they closed the door?

The sound of a drawer being pulled open had him gazing at Elizabeth. She held a white ornament which, by the fine, gold handiwork, he concluded was French.

She stared at him, her entire demeanor changed. Before, she had been acting like a scared rabbit, her gaze never settling on one thing and talking so fast it made Edward's head hurt. But now she stood straight-backed and glared at him as if she was angry with him.

Was she mad? Was that why his mother had no concern for the propriety of the situation? Mayhap she knew James would be sending Elizabeth away to an asylum. Pain shot through his heart at that. Even if she were insane, he could not ignore his love for her. Mayhap he could care for her and mayhap he could help her return to her normal self in time.

He stood up slowly, afraid of scaring her. "Elizabeth. Are you unwell?"

She gazed at the ornament. "No, Edward, I am not unwell, at least not in the way you mean it. But I am angry that you have decided that is what's wrong with me. Do you think I'm mad?"

"Of course not. Mayhap you have overextended yourself today. Did James and my mother hurt you in any way?"

"No, and stop being silly. I am not hurt. I am not unwell. What we have told you is the truth. I am not from this time; I am from your future."

"I can't believe that, but I can believe you believe it." He paced to the window and turned to face her. She looked so serious, her eyes pleading for him to believe her, believe *in* her. And his heart wanted to, but his mind knew it was an impossibility. Although he wanted to take her into his arms, protect her for all time, love her, his finger stroked his jawline. He needed to calm her down. Mayhap if he played along. "Tell me about your time."

She gave him a quizzical look then laughed. "You're going to psychoanalyze me? Really? Okay, fine. Do your best, boyo." She thought for a moment. "Oh, I know, how about we start with my family."

Edward kept his face calm and gave her a small nod. He didn't want to upset her any more than she was already, and he definitely didn't want her speech to get any stranger. He was finding it difficult enough to understand her as it was. His lips twitched but he contained the smile. She was so beautiful, so adamant, so passionate.

"There's Mom and Dad, of course. Whom you've met?"

Edward's lips tightened at the commoners' names for her parents, but he nodded.

"Didn't you think they were strange?"

"Not that I can remember. They were sensibly attired and spoke extremely well. On the few occasions I met them, they..." he paused. "I withdraw my earlier comments. They were indeed strange; in fact, Dianne congratulated me on a grape harvest before I'd even decided to think about growing a vineyard."

A flash of confusion washed over Elizabeth's face, then she beamed at him. "There, you see?"

"No."

"They traveled so often, they must have forgotten what time they were in." She wrapped her arms around her chest in a hug. "That means they are coming back in your future, sometime when you do have a good harvest. Oh, Edward, you should have thought about that and asked them more questions. Instead, you had to be a gentleman and let the whole episode go." She shook her head. "Do you believe me now?"

He was certain his own confusion showed on his face. Could it be possible? He wanted to believe her, but nothing in his education supported such an outlandish idea. "I don't know."

She rounded the desk and stood before him, holding the ornament in front of his face. "This is the time travel device, and all I have to do is turn the top here, so the leaves align, and I will disappear forever. Do you want me to go?"

He placed his hands on her shoulders and pierced her with his gaze. "No. I think I would die if I never saw—never touched—you again." He gazed at her mouth and when the tip of her tongue appeared and wet her lips, he lost his mind and kissed her, pausing only to ask, "Please, Elizabeth, make me believe."

Elizabeth broke the kiss first and backed away. "First things first. Your mother knows. Shouldn't you at least trust her?"

He tried to look her in the eyes, but his gaze kept going back to her lips. "My mother has been known to gammon before."

She glanced from one of Edward's hands to the other. He tightened his jaw and withdrew his hands from her shoulders.

"Okay then, I'll tell you about my sister. Abby is the oldest of the Davis children and she was the first to use the orb, albeit accidentally."

"Orb?"

She shook the ornament. "That's what we call this. Anyway, she went to Scotland and met a handsome laird. They fell in love and he believed her about her being from the future. He was much more open-minded than you are, I guess. She stayed with him. That's where she is now. On the island of Orpol in 1746."

"How can that be?"

She huffed. "Because, I told you, we can time travel. There's another orb at home and my sister, brother, and I travelled back to Scotland past and that's how we found out Abby was staying with her laird. In fact, I wouldn't be surprised if my brother and sister turned up here. They could, you know?"

Edward rubbed his face with his palms. "Please stop."

He strode to the window and, keeping his back to her, gazed unseeingly at the hazy vista ahead. Why was she prolonging the charade? Or did she believe her own lies? Had he been mistaken? Was she mad? Questions were all he had, and no answers were forthcoming. More questions crowded his mind. How could she think an orb, a piece of frippery, could take her backwards and forwards in time? Or was she part of a larger masquerade? Had the duke put her up to this? He tightened his lips. The duke had announced he and Edward's mother were to be married in the same breath as he'd told him Elizabeth was from the future.

He drew in a deep breath. So that was their game. To keep him in a state of confusion so he could not dwell on the duke's announcement. They knew he would not countenance such a liaison when the whole of England believed Chodstone to be affianced to Elizabeth. But why would Elizabeth agree to such a thing?

He rubbed his face, dragging his hand down his cheeks. Her parents had indeed been wholly out of tune with English society, and Mrs Davis had commented on his harvest in passing, but that was all it was, a comment in passing. As he surmised at the time, she had confused him with someone else of her acquaintance.

He threw a glance over his shoulder. Elizabeth still stood in the same place, staring at him with worried eyes as she continually twisted and turned the orb in front of her and chewed on her bottom lip. His stomach twisted at the thought that she would damage her beautiful lip. He sighed and turned to face her, wanting more than anything else for her to renounce her proclamation and confide in him of his mother and the duke's prevarications.

"Will you please admit your duplicity and that of my mother and Chodstone?"

She shook her head.

"How could you think I could believe such a thing? The very thought of an orb, an ornament, taking people through time is absurd."

She bit her lip harder and Edward thought he could make out a spot of blood under her teeth. He rubbed at a pain that formed in his chest and turned back to the window. He had come there ready to announce his love for her, ready to fight for her, to the death if the duke called him to a duel. He would have done anything to have her by his side for all time. He frowned. All time. She could not be sincere in her affections if she persisted with the gammon and he would not entertain such flights of fancy. He would prefer to live alone than with a woman he could not trust.

Izzy's heart sank at the stiffness of Edward's back. He did not believe her, and she could not marry him if he didn't. It was just too big of a barrier, and she was certain that living intimately with him, she would not be able to keep up the American socialite persona she had carefully woven up to that point. She had to have a refuge, a safe place where she could be herself, a place where she could be herself with him—otherwise there was no point. He would either think she was mad or she herself would go mad trying to live two lives.

Surely faith and honesty were essential to a durable relationship, and she needed to know she could share anything with him, to tell him things not meant for others' ears, to trust he would believe her when others might not.

"Edward," she whispered, and he turned. She stilled her hands and clasped the orb tightly, straightening her back. "You must believe me. I could not in all good conscience marry you if you did not know the truth."

He opened his mouth, but Izzy hurried on. "No, please, just listen. I am from the future, as were my parents before me. That is how I came to be the duke's ward. My parents have many contacts whom they trust with their secret throughout time. The duke was their contact in this era and so he became mine. I didn't know your mother knew about my parents, not until a few weeks ago anyway, but I am so glad she does. It makes everything much easier."

Izzy gazed into his dark eyes and sensed the coldness there. Her heart sank into her stomach, but she lifted her chin and continued. "Why can't you just believe me? Do you not love me enough? I thought we had a connection, a deep understanding that nothing would be too much for us to believe of one another. We need trust if we are to go on, Edward. Listen, can you at least imagine that time travel is possible? I am from the future, a future where electricity is in every household, where cars—horseless wagons—can go over one hundred miles an hour and are driven through streets and along highways that connect town to city. We have buildings that are over one hundred stories high—some, way more— and planes that fly through the sky from country to country in hours."

Edward narrowed his eyes at her last statement and held up his hands, palms out. "Stop, Elizabeth. I cannot imagine such things and I refuse to hear any more nonsense."

Blast, Izzy thought. Maybe she had gone too far. By the dark look on his face, she guessed he thought she was insane. Tears burnt the back of her eyes, but she refused to let them fall. She blinked them back and drew in a deep breath. It would seem they were at an impasse.

He looked at her as if he had never seen her before let alone kissed her. The memory of his kisses flooded through her every cell and she gazed intently at him, hoping he remembered them as well. Blast him, she loved him. After thinking she would spend the rest of her life with the man, how could she now live without him? No, she could not live a lie, she could not pretend to be someone she wasn't, not with Edward. How could she bear to lose him? A sharp pain pierced her heart. She gasped.

His eyes hardened even more, and without thinking, she squeezed and twisted the orb with both hands. Everything went black and she fell.

The last thought she had was that her heart had broken, and she had died. Familiar lights pierced her lids and she opened her eyes. She wasn't dead: she was back in the house, back in the basement, back home.

EDWARD GASPED. ELIZABETH HAD DISAPPEARED BEFORE HIS very eyes. Staring at the rug that she had been standing on only a second before, his mind swirled. He opened his mouth to speak but no words came out of his dry throat. He swallowed. "What trickery is this?"

He spun full circle. "Elizabeth. I know you are hiding somewhere. Come out this instant."

The room was silent. Only his short, sharp breaths sounded in his ears. The only answer his mired mind could bring forth was that she was an illusionist's accomplice, mayhap using Edward for sport.

He rushed out of the room and into the foyer, shouting, "Elizabeth. Miss Davis."

He looked everywhere but could not find her or her guardian. He made his way to the second floor, where he met Hampton and two housemaids.

"I'm sorry, my lord, but I cannot allow you to enter the duke's private quarters without his order."

"I'm looking for Miss Davis. Is she here?"

Hampton glanced at the two maids, who shook their heads. "She isn't here, my lord."

Edward tightened his jaw. "She must be. Why are you hiding her?"

"We are not hiding her, my lord. Miss Davis is not upstairs."

"Then she must be downstairs." Edward wheeled around on his heels and descended the stairs.

One of the maids called after him. "I was just there, my lord, and the miss was nowhere to be seen."

Edward glanced back at the three of them. He sighed. They were telling the truth and by the surprised, but wary, looks on their faces, he decided to not take issue with their words.

They obviously thought him numb-brained, and soon the whole of London town would hear of his ramblings.

He clumped down the stairs and sat down heavily on the bottom step. Covering his face with his hands, he tried to make sense of what had just happened.

Edward didn't know how long he had been sitting there, recalling the moment Elizabeth disappeared from his life, but the click-clack of a man's boots pushed the recollection from his mind. The sound of the boots stopped close by. Edward dragged his hands down his face and looked up.

"Chodstone."

"Why are you sitting on my staircase and not with Elizabeth?"

"She is gone."

"Gone? Where? Speak up, Wellsneath, you are not making sense."

Edward narrowed his eyes at Chodstone. "You know where she is, don't you?"

"What are you talking about?"

"Is she with Mother?"

"The last we saw of her, she was with you."

"She disappeared."

"What?"

Edward noted the duke's quick glance to the open sitting room doors. He stood up and rounded on the duke. "You know where she is. Tell me."

The duke pushed Edward aside and strode into the sitting room, and Edward followed.

The man went directly to his escritoire and, slamming his

palms on the top, glared at Edward. "What did you say to her?"

"I could not believe what she said. I knew it was a ruse, but she would not confess."

"You stupid man. She was telling you the truth and now it appears you have not only broken her heart, but you have chased her back to her time. Now I will never have the chance to say my proper goodbyes. I thought you more intelligent, Wellsneath. But in fact, you are as small-minded and unaccepting as the rest of society. There is more to this world than balls and fashions and gossip."

Edward stood erect. Good grief, could it be true after all? The duke was adamant, and his very own mother surely would not put on such a gammon.

He took the calling-out he himself knew he deserved. That and more. Mayhap it was the truth. Mayhap Elizabeth was from a future time. He gave a small shake of his head. If that was so, he would never see her again. "She said you were her contact in this time. Can you not contact her?"

"No. She and the orb, the time travel device, have gone for good."

Edward fell into the armchair, his body suddenly too weak to stand.

Chodstone sat at the desk, and both stared unseeingly ahead in silence.

Hot tears slid from Edward's eyes and he cared not. He had lost his Elizabeth for all time. He started and swiped away the tears. "Time."

Chodstone blinked. "What?"

"Time. If she is in the future, I can send her a missive." He stood up and gazed at the duke. "Will you help me?"

CHAPTER 27

Izzy waited for the sense of movement to stop, and once it did, she looked up. Bree, smiling down at her from her perch on a stool.

"Hey, Izzy, you okay?"

Izzy got to her feet. "I guess." She wiped the wet from under her eyes.

Bree hopped off the stool and hugged Izzy. "You've been crying. Want to talk about it?"

Izzy nodded but couldn't talk around the lump that lodged in her throat.

"Don't say anything yet. I'll get Max and Garrett, so you don't have to repeat anything."

Bree ran up the stairs and was back with Garrett and Max in tow before Izzy had settled into her surroundings.

"Izzy," Max said, throwing her arms around her and giving her a hug. She let go and stepped back. "You shouldn't have gone like that. We were worried about you."

"I'm glad you're back safe and sound," Garrett said, giving her a one-armed side hug. "But the outcome could have been very different. You could have been killed or stuck in the past somewhere. Where did you go, anyway?"

"Eighteen-twelve England."

"You've been crying," Max said.

Izzy automatically wiped her eyes. "It's a long story."

"Here, sit down." Bree pointed to a sitting area that hadn't been there before Izzy left. Two comfortable blue sofas separated by a low coffee table sat on a blue-and-cream rug in the corner of the basement.

Izzy sat down on the nearest sofa. "Who did this?"

"Me," Max said, sitting next to Izzy. "We spend so much time down here, I thought we might as well have somewhere comfortable to sit."

Bree and Garrett sat on the opposite sofa and gazed at Izzy.

Izzy told them everything, the whole story from the moment she'd met Edward to the moment she'd left him. While she spoke, Max held her hand and squeezed every now and then if Izzy got too distraught.

"Good riddance," Garrett said. "He doesn't sound like someone I'd like anyway."

"Why?" Max asked. "Because he didn't believe Izzy? How soon we forget, huh? You refused to believe Mom and Dad until we were in the past with Abby."

Garrett shrugged, stood up, and stretched. "I'm sorry, Iz, but I'm going to bed. Hope you feel better in the morning."

Bree sat back spreading her arms over the back of the sofa. "You can always go back, you know?"

"I don't think that's a good idea," Max said.

"Max is right," Izzy said. "I can't go back, not with Edward not only *not* believing me but probably thinking I'm stark raving mad."

Max yawned. "It's late. Let's all go to bed and see how we feel in the morning."

IZZY SIPPED HER MORNING CUP OF COFFEE, TRYING PUSH the dreams of Edward that had haunted her sleep out of her mind. She glanced at the door and wondered where everyone was. She hoped they were making breakfast, because all of a sudden, her stomach felt as empty as her heart.

Garrett and Max were glad but surprised to have Izzy home, but Bree didn't seem surprised at all that she had returned. In fact, Izzy thought, frowning at the pile of paper on the dining table that was her book manuscript, Bree seemed to have been waiting for her.

She pushed the hard copy of her manuscript to the side. There was no way she could concentrate on editing the stupid thing, not when she knew it didn't have the happy ending, she had been looking forward to writing.

Max came into the dining room, carrying a plate stacked high with toast and jam.

"Sorry, it's all I could come up with. Garrett's gone riding and Bree took off early."

"Where did she go?"

"Town. And don't ask why, because I don't know."

Izzy bit into a piece of toast. "This is good, thanks."

"It's probably all for the best, you know? I mean, it's better to find out now that Edward doesn't have your back, rather than later."

"Maybe you're right, but I can't get him out of my mind." She took another bite and chewed. "I love him, Maxi."

Max's mouth pulled down at the corners in sympathy. "I won't give you any platitudes. Just know I'm here for you."

"Thanks."

They ate the rest of their sweet breakfast in silence.

Max finished her toast and stood up. "Although you shouldn't have taken off like that in the first place, you're back now, so you can help us clean up the attic. We need somewhere to store our stuff. You wouldn't believe how much junk is up there."

Izzy knew. She had spent quite a lot of time up there before she left what seemed a lifetime ago. She sighed.

With Max gone, Izzy was alone, and the silence began to close in. Izzy eyed her manuscript. *Why couldn't you be the man I needed? Why couldn't you just believe me and hold me and tell me you never wanted me to go?* She leapt up to her feet. *I may as well help.*

Izzy put all her effort into cleaning and organizing the attic. She cooked lunch and dinner, and by the time the day ended, she was exhausted. Climbing into bed, she thought she just might have a chance of sleeping.

But no, Edward wouldn't leave her alone. His smiling face stayed in her mind no matter what else she tried to think about. The memory of his kisses, how they made her feel, how the sensations still whirled around her body as if he were right there in her bedroom.

She tried to think about Bree. Where was she exactly? She had called earlier and said she met up with a friend and was staying in town for the night. She told Izzy not to do anything rash until she got back. Why? What was she up to? Now wide awake, Izzy's senses were on high alert. What did she expect Izzy to do?

Mayhap... Izzy let out a snort. She wasn't in Regency England any longer, so she had to stop using their funny expressions.

Maybe Bree expected Izzy to use the orb again, but there was no way she would. Edward didn't love her enough to believe in her when she needed him to. Her stomach twisted as his smiling face changed to stone, and cold, hard coal took the place of his eyes. She wondered what he thought when she'd disappeared. Did he believe her at last? Was he sorry she had gone? Or was he relieved? Relieved to not have to cope with such nonsense? Not to have to deal with a mad woman?

Izzy awoke to pounding on her bedroom door. What time was it? She was sure she'd only just fallen to sleep.

The pounding continued.

She sat up and rubbed her eyes. "Wait!"

Grabbing her housecoat, she slid off the bed. The curtains were open, and stars glinted in the still night sky. Who would be up so early?

The rapping on the door continued and Izzy pulled the door open. Bree's fist came at her face, and she instinctively clasped her cousin's wrist. "What are you doing?"

"Trying to wake you, of course." Bree pulled her hand back and, nudging Izzy out of the way, breezed into the room and plonked down on the bed. She waved an envelope in the air. "Sorry, Iz, but I've been waiting for this all night."

Izzy peered at the letter. The paper was yellow with age. "What's that?"

Patting the bed beside her, Bree grinned. "Come on, you'll want to sit down before you read it."

"Just tell me, Bree. I'm in no mood for your games. I'm tired and want to get back to sleep."

Her cousin shook the letter. "This will wake you up. Come on, stop being a spoilsport and sit down."

Izzy gave an impatient huff. Bree had always been a bit eccentric, but she'd never woken Izzy up in the middle of the night before. "Okay then." She sat down beside Bree. "Give it to me."

Bree handed her the envelope with a mischievous grin.

Izzy narrowed her eyes at her cousin but quickly read the

front aloud. "Miss Elizabeth Davis, care of Mr Carter Martenell. You got this from Carter?"

Bree nodded. "Open it."

Izzy turned the letter over. The seal was the Earl of Wellsneath's stamp. "It can't be," she breathed. Her hands shook as she used her fingernail and pried the seal off. She withdrew a sheet of aged cream paper that smelled musty. She unfolded it and glanced at Bree.

Bree kept grinning and nodding. "Read it."

Recognizing Edward's writing, Izzy tried to take in the entire letter in one glance. She caught all the words she wanted to hear more than life itself. *Love you, want you, forgive me, believe you.*

"Read it out loud," Bree said.

Izzy clasped the page to her chest and shook her head. Tears pooled in her eyes. "Can you send me back?"

Without waiting for Bree to reply, she ran out of the room and down into the basement. She grabbed the orb she had left on the bench the night before.

Bree was hot on her heels. "Wait!"

"I wasn't going to turn it. I know you have to set the black orb first."

"That's not what I was stopping you for. You need to change first, dummy."

Izzy looked down at her short, pink nightie. Blast. The clothes she'd worn in the past were in her room and she didn't have time to search the wardrobe for another outfit.

Bree must have guessed Izzy's problem. She grabbed a blue maxi coat off the coat rack and threw it at Izzy. "Put this on. It'll have to do."

She fiddled with the black orb and gazed at Izzy. "I can't be a hundred percent sure you'll arrive when you left. I know it won't be before then, but I'm not sure how close it'll be."

Izzy crammed Edward's letter in the coat pocket. "So long as it's the same year."

"Don't worry, it's the same year."

Izzy picked up the white orb and twisted the top. "Wish me luck."

She didn't hear if Bree did or not, because she was once again propelled through time and space.

Izzy must have become used to time traveling because, as the blackness evaporated, her previous vertigo was gone, and she landed on stable legs in her bedroom in the duke's house. She looked around. The room was still the same, although the bedding had been removed from the bed. She sat on the chair at her desk and withdrew the letter from her coat pocket. She whispered the written words her heart ached to hear:

"My dearest Elizabeth,

"Please don't throw this letter away without reading every word."

I wouldn't do that.

"I watched you disappear before my very eyes and it broke my heart. Not that I could blame you for leaving me, but I was such a dolt that I could not believe and trust in the only woman I have ever loved. And I do love you, Elizabeth, with every ounce of my soul, I love you."

Izzy wiped the tears away so she could see better.

"Please forgive me, my love. I believe you, believe in you. You are my world, and my world in this time is forever bereft without you.

"Chodstone assures me you will receive this letter, but I am fearful he is too optimistic. However, if you do, please know I love you, I believe you, I want you with me for all time. Please come back to me.

"Yours always for all time,"

Izzy sniffed.

"Edward"

She placed the letter on the desk and sobbed. "Oh, Edward."

Pulling out a drawer, she picked up a handkerchief. It was clean but it didn't smell freshly laundered. In fact—she turned around and gazed over the room anew—the air was stale.

She stood up. How did she not notice that before? How much time had passed?

She wiped her face with the handkerchief and stared at her red, swollen eyes in the small mirror. "Are you still waiting for me, Edward? Or have you gone on with your life?"

She leapt up and hurried to the window. Drawing the curtains, she squinted at the sun's brightness. Guessing it to be late morning, she pulled her coat about her, raced out of the room, and heading to the stairs, came face to face with Lucy.

"Lucy!"

"Miss, oh miss, it is good to see you back."

"Back? How long have I been gone?"

Lucy narrowed her eyes. "You do not know?"

"Just tell me, Lucy, how long?"

"Three months and a sennight."

Izzy sucked on her bottom lip. Over three months. What if Edward had started seeing Vera again? What if he hadn't waited for her?

She pushed past Lucy. "Where's the duke?"

"In the front sitting room, miss."

Izzy hit Lucy playfully. "Izzy," she insisted, and hurried to the front room. She stopped dead. He and Alice were taking tea and chatting happily. "James?"

He looked up and glanced at Alice, who twisted around and peered over the back of the sofa. They both stood up.

"Elizabeth!" they said in unison and hurried to her side. Alice was the first to hug her. "You're back."

She stepped to the side to give James room.

James picked Izzy up and swung her around. "I knew you would return." He put her down and pulled the cord that summoned the butler.

"Come sit down and tell us what has happened in your life."

Once they sat down, Izzy told them about going back to the future and about how her cousin had brought her a letter from Edward.

"Ah," James said when she was finished. "So, you got it then."

"Yes. How is he? Where is he?"

Alice took her hand in hers. "He has been in a state these last months. There was no speaking to him. He didn't even come to our wedding."

"You're married?"

They threw loving glances at one another. "For two months now," James said, smiling at his wife.

Hampton stood on the threshold and bowed. "You called, Your Grace?"

Izzy noted a look of surprise on Hampton's face when his gaze passed by her, but he quickly concealed it.

"Yes," James said. "Have the carriage brought around to the front immediately."

"Yes, Your Grace."

"The carriage?" Izzy asked.

"You will need it to go to Wellsneath House."

"Wellsneath House?"

"That is where Edward is," Alice said. "That or mayhap, Gentleman Sam's. No, I am sure he is at Wellsneath House today."

Izzy leapt out of the carriage and raced up the stairs. She banged the door knocker as hard as she could until the door opened.

Larson, Edward's butler, dipped his head. "Miss Davis, I am sorry, but the earl isn't taking visitors at this time."

Izzy pushed past him. "He'll see me."

"But miss."

"Edward! Edward," she called, then rounded on the butler. "Where is he?"

Larson stared at her.

"He's in the library, miss."

He moved to take the lead to the library, but Izzy stopped him by pulling on the back of his coat. "No, you stay here. I know the way."

Not knocking, Izzy opened the door to the library and stepped over the threshold. Edward mustn't have heard the door open, because he didn't look up from the open account book on his desk. Her soft slippers didn't make a sound on the thick rug as she walked purposefully toward him. She stopped at the desk and sighed. She had thought him hard at work on his accounts, but on closer inspection, he was scrawling doodles across the pages of numbers.

He either heard her sigh or sensed someone was there, but he didn't look up as he spoke. "I am busy. Go away."

"Edward."

He looked up, closed his eyes and shook his head, snapped his eyes open again and leapt to his feet. The chair under him tumbled over. "Elizabeth?"

He stared at her as if he thought she might be a ghost or an apparition.

She gave him a shaky smile. "It's me."

Rounding the desk, he stood before her, his gaze flitting from her eyes to her hair, to her mouth, to her chin, to her eyes. "It is you."

Izzy smiled and nodded. "How are you?"

"Pleasantries? I am in no mood for pleasantries."

He gently held her face in his hands and the heavy emotion in his dark gaze had her heart flipping.

"You came back," he whispered.

"I got your letter."

He laughed. "You got my letter and you came back to me. I am not certain I can believe the truth of it." He kissed her forehead. "You feel real. Are you real, my love?"

Izzy wrapped her arms around the back of his neck and whispered close to his mouth. "I'm real."

She didn't know if she initiated the kiss or if he did, but in less than a second, they were kissing one another like they would die if parted, only coming up for air or to speak in husky tones. "Forgive me, my love," Edward groaned. "I cannot live without you."

His hands roamed over her back, stopped to pull her in closer to his body, sending shivers of pleasure through her. "I can't live without you either." Izzy could hardly talk; he had completely taken her every breath away.

"I love you."

"Oh, Edward, I love you."

He pressed kisses all over her face, her chin, and her neck. She groaned and he caught her mouth with his once more. Izzy tried to get closer, to feel every movement of muscle in his chest, to feel her heart beating in rhythm with his.

Edward finally pulled back and enveloped her with his passionate gaze. "Will you marry me, Miss Davis? Will you be mine for all time?"

"For all time," she moaned, pulling him back and covering his mouth with hers.

EPILOGUE

I zzy turned full circle in front of the small mirror. From what she could see, the pale cream dress fit perfectly, and the hand-knitted yellow daisies around the neckline and hem were stunning. Blonde tendrils framed her face and Lucy had intertwined tiny buttercup-yellow flowers in her hair. The abigail had outdone herself. The effect was magical and just for that moment in time, she felt like the most beautiful woman in the world.

"You look wonderful." Lucy said, fiddling with a stray curl around Izzy's ear.

Izzy brushed her hand away. "It's fine. No, it's perfect. Thank you."

Lucy grinned. "The earl is going to think you're so cool."

Izzy laughed. Lucy had decided to learn as many modern terms as she could, and she loved the word cool and all it stood for. "Be careful not to say anything like that around the *haut ton.*"

"I won't, Izzy."

"Good girl. Should we be going now?"

James had transported everyone to his country estate and

arranged for her and Edward to be married in Chodstone's very own chapel. It was just too romantic, and suddenly, Izzy's heart flipped full circle in her chest. How could she be so lucky? Edward was the most wonderful man in existence, and he wanted to spend the rest of his life with her, and only her.

"If we don't go now, we'll be late, and I don't want Edward thinking I've stood him up."

Lucy shook her head and held up Izzy's coat.

"I don't want to cover up this beautiful dress."

"It'll be chilly until you get inside the chapel."

Izzy put on the coat and waited for Lucy to move, but she just stood there smiling at Izzy.

"Well?" Izzy said.

"His Grace said to wait here for him."

Her heart picked up its pace and Izzy rubbed her clammy hands together. "What's the time?"

Lucy hurried out of the room to check the big wooden clock at the end of the hall.

Her face was beaming when she returned. "Fifteen minutes past the hour."

"What hour?"

"Nine."

"Why are you so happy about that? We are supposed to be there at nine thirty. It's at least ten minutes to the chapel. We'll be late." Her voice rose an octave as she spoke.

"It's cool."

"Not funny, Lucy."

A knock sounded and the door opened before Lucy could get to it, not that she actually moved a muscle to do so.

In walked Max and Garrett.

Izzy let out a cry and hugged them to her, laughing and crying with joy at the same time. "How? When? Did James know?" She let them go and gazed from one sibling to the other. "I thought I'd never see you again."

Max, dressed in a pretty blue day dress, smiled and shrugged. "Apparently, we're not only connected by blood, but by time. Somehow the orbs know where and when we all are at all times."

Izzy frowned. "How?"

Garrett pulled at his neck scarf and tilted his head toward Lucy. "Is it okay to talk?"

"Yes, Lucy isn't just my maid, she's my friend. She knows everything."

"And I think it's so cool," Lucy said.

Max let out a laugh. "I see you've been educating her."

"Yes." Izzy gave Lucy a hard look. "But she knows to not say things like that if we're not alone."

Lucy nodded.

"So how do the orbs know?" Izzy wanted to know.

"We haven't a clue, but Bree said Mom and Dad told her, so it must be true."

"She knows more than she tells us," Izzy said. "Where is she anyway?"

"She didn't come. Just like with Abby, she said she couldn't spare the time away."

"Except," Max said. "I'm pretty sure she can set the time devices to any time she wants."

"Mayhap she is frightened to travel through time," Lucy said.

Izzy turned and stared at her abigail, and Max said, "You are extremely insightful, and I think you may be right. Although she says she has to go back in time, too, she doesn't seem to be in any hurry to go."

Garrett leaned his shoulder on the wall and crossed his ankles. "I think I'm going to have a nice long talk to Bree when we get back."

"Izzy?" a voice called from the hall.

"Abby?" Izzy ran out of the room and stopped abruptly.

"Abby," she cried and, immediately covering the distance between them, threw her arms around her eldest sister. "Oh, Abby, Abby."

Abby laughed and hugged Izzy. "It's so good to see you."

Izzy didn't want to let her go but she had to see her, so she pulled back. "I can't believe it. How did Bree get you here?"

"She sent the black orb back with a note to dress up for a Regency wedding, and here we are."

Izzy said, "I don't care how Bree did it, but this is the happiest day of my life."

She only just then noticed Iain standing back, watching them.

He smiled. "Hello, Elizabeth."

Izzy hugged him. "Are you still looking after my big sister?"

He glanced at Abby. "I am."

Max's high-pitched cry startled Izzy for a second, but she moved out of the way so her sisters could hug.

And then they were all out in the hall, hugging and laughing and crying. Garrett shook Iain's hand rapidly. Iain gave him a one-armed hug. "It is good to see ye, Garrett. My sister would like to know if ye are well."

Izzy could have sworn Garrett blushed.

"I am very well," he said. "But don't we have a wedding to get to?"

"Changing the subject, little brother?" Max asked.

"He's right," Izzy said. "Edward will be wondering where I am. Ooh, I can't wait for you all to meet him. He's amazing."

"Don't listen to him, Garrett," Abby said. "Maeve has enough beaus without you."

Garrett grinned. "I'm not surprised, but none like me, I bet."

"Lucy," Izzy called.

"Here." She handed Izzy her reticule.

Lucy smiled at everyone.

"Where's your coat? Hurry up, we have to go."

"Me?"

Izzy took her arm. "You think I'd get married and not have my BFF with me?"

JAMES AND ALICE HAD SPARED NO EXPENSE ON THE wedding breakfast. The wall that separated the reception rooms had been removed, making one big ballroom. A small orchestra played at the end of the second room. They had left space between the pit and the dining tables so everyone could dance.

Izzy looked around the tables. She didn't know how Bree had been able to get everyone there, but she was glad her cousin had. Abby and Iain were chatting happily to Max, and Garrett was laughing at what Alice was saying. Izzy caught James's name more than once, and guessed it was a story that probably shouldn't be told.

Edward placed his hand over Izzy's. "Are you happy?"

"I am. Do you like my family?"

"I do." He chuckled. "They are wonderfully strange, and I can see how much they love you." He took her hands in his. "However, no one can love you as much as I, and I do, my love, for all time."

Before his mouth fully closed down on hers, Izzy whispered. "For all time."

FROM CALLIE

Thank you for reading *From Bars to Ballrooms*!
Book III in The Time Orb Series, *From Cafés to Cossacks*, is
available at your preferred store now.
And... if you'd like to learn about new releases in the series
and have the chance to grab *Henrietta's Dance*, a Regency
Romance Novella, please head over to my website and join
my newsletter.
https://callieberkham.com/
I value our friendship and will never share your email, ever.
And don't worry if you have already joined my mailing list
because all the free books will be added to my newsletter as I
write them.

More books by Callie
The Time Orb Series:
From Suits to Kilts
From Bars to Ballrooms
From Cafés to Cossacks